BOOK TH

Robert Ryan

Cover design by www.damonza.com

ISBN: 9781697015034
(print edition)

Trotting Fox Press

Contents

1. The Broken Sword   3
2. Will You Serve the Land?   8
3. The Tomb   13
4. Homecoming   17
5. A Time of Change   21
6. The Witch   26
7. All the World is Yours   33
8. Is it True?   41
9. A New Banner   51
10. Like Whey from Curds   55
11. He Would be a King   62
12. The Old Masters   67
13. Nothing is Destined   75
14. Only by Chance   81
15. Not my Heritage   86
16. A Long Night   90
17. Ambush   97
18. The Enemy   109
19. Five Tribes   117
20. There Goes a Good Man   125
21. The Golden God   130
22. Let Them March to Us   134
23. I Will Not Kneel   139
24. First Blood is Spilled   146
25. Worthy of That Axe   150
26. Like A Torch   164
27. The Hunter Becomes the Hunted   169
28. Advance!   177
29. Free of Ambition   183
Epilogue   190
Appendix: Encyclopedic Glossary   194

1. The Broken Sword

Brand walked silently through the sacred woods of the Duthenor, and the magic within him grew restless. It sensed something, and responded.

He stepped carefully and reverently, for this was not a place to move fast or to speak. And those few with him did the same.

Shorty and Taingern were among them. What they thought of this place, he did not know. But they each had seen strange things before, and knew there were powers in the world beyond the understanding of people. This was such a site where those powers were strong, and the ancient Duthenor had known it.

The Duthenor seldom came here. It was a place of ancient ceremony, and usually it was left alone except for certain times of the year and certain occasions.

This was one such occasion. The sword of the chieftains of the Duthenor was broken. It was a link between father and son from a time out of memory and into myth. It was a part of the Duthenor people themselves. It was a symbol of them, and its breaking was like the dying of a chieftain.

And there were rites that went with that, born from a past older even than the Duthenor habitation of the Duthgar. They went back to the dark days, the time of the elù-haraken. The Shadowed Wars.

One of those rites was the offering of something of great value back to the land from whence all life sprang. In this case, it would be the sword itself.

Brand carried the broken shards reverently in his hands, held palm up before him. No steel blade was allowed in the sacred woods, and none of his companions carried a weapon. But the broken sword was the offering itself, and there was a tradition of giving swords back to the land when their owner died. This was in that spirit.

Though it was early morning, the forest was dark about him. The trees were mostly pine, and the scent of resin sharpened the air. To all sides the trunks marched away, dark and mysterious. Branches creaked, and strange sounds of wood rubbing against wood disturbed the quiet.

It was an eerie place, and Brand sensed foreboding tickle the back of his neck. Was that the natural effect of the strange woods? Or were his instincts warning him of something?

It did not matter. They were nearly at their destination now, and there was no turning back. With him and his two oldest friends came Sighern and several of the highest-ranking lords of both the Duthenor and Callenor tribes.

Brand paused. Then his gaze found the hidden path that he remembered of old, and he turned down it. Overgrown by ancient trees it was, and the sense of eeriness increased. Here, he remembered coming once as a child with his father. It had been eerie then too. Strange that it should be even more so now as an adult.

Furthgil, the gray-bearded lord of the Callenor, preeminent among his tribe now that Gormengil was dead, cast a wary gaze about him as he followed down the dark trail. Well he might. No Callenor had been here before, but they too would have their sacred place. Behind him, for there was only room for one man at a time, came the lords Brodruin and Garvengil. These were the most senior surviving nobility of the Duthenor. They hid their unease well, but they had been here before and knew what to expect. Last, but not least, came Bruidiger. No lord at

4

all, but a warrior of great presence. He represented the Norvinor tribe, and Brand thought it fitting. Here he had gathered, against tradition in such a sacred place, not only the Duthenor but representatives of all the peoples that faced the great threat to come. It was the beginnings of binding them into a single force, and that was needed. Without it, they would not survive.

The path wound downhill now, and the steepness made each step treacherous. It grew darker, and the trees leaned over them, looking down like sentries, scrutinizing those who passed.

But pass they did, and they came to their destination. The trees gave way, grudgingly. The land leveled, and a patch of clear sky, blue-purple as it seemed looking up through the dark tunnel of tree trunks that formed a circle around them, gazed down unblinking like an eye.

Here of old the chieftains of the Duthenor made offerings to the land to honor it. Here was the *Ferstellenpund*, a tarn of still water, mirrorlike, its surface still and the bright-colored sky reflected in it. At night, there would be stars, but no offerings were ever made save by daylight.

The banks were too steep to walk, but the end of the trail had led down a rocky path to the water's edge and a flat shore. The path was cut into the rock by the hand of man, but no Duthenor would ever have done that. To the shore Brand came, the others behind him. And here, by the very edge of the tarn, they halted amid a heavy silence. This was where he would commit the sword back to the land. This was the sacred heart of the woods.

Tendrils of mist reached up from the water, creeping into the trees. No sound came to Brand's ears. The whole world seemed watchful, as though it awaited some event. It was a dreary place, and Brand's heart was heavy. He began to think that the eeriness of the woods was caused by his own emotion. Grief washed through him. So many had died recently. So many more yet would. And the sword of his forefathers was broken, even as his parents were dead. The hopes of his youth were ash, and the reality of the world was hard to bear.

But bear it he must. He straightened. For now, he would do what was required of a chieftain. When he left these woods, the combined army of the Duthenor and Callenor tribes would be waiting nearby. He would lead them, and he would wield them like a weapon to do what had to be done.

A movement caught his eye. It was a trickle of water running down the stony bank at the other side of the pond. But there was no sound of running water, nor did it disturb the surface. It was strange. Yet there were many strange things about the pond. Another was that no one had ever plumbed its depths. And it had been tried, at least according to legend.

Brand gave no more thought to it. He uttered the sacred words of the Duthenor, the words handed down from father to son, from chieftain to chieftain, since days beyond memory. They were the words spoken at an offering. They were the words spoken at a chieftain's funeral. And he heard an intake of breath from the men of the other tribes with him. They would have their own such sacred words, and they would know the sanctity of such things. They would know that Brand was treating them as lords of the Duthenor, letting them hear what only lords of the Duthenor had ever heard before.

And when he was done, he cast the shards of the broken blade into the center of the pond. The still water shattered. The image of the sky shuddered, and the water showed the flashing image of the surrounding trees, leaping and striding like warriors drawing swords to attack.

The shards of the blade slid into the water, disappearing from sight, though even that made no noise, and it troubled Brand.

Yet the offering was made. That which was drawn from the earth was laid to rest within it again. The land had been thanked, and the rite completed. It was time to turn and go.

But Brand did not move. Where the water should be going still again, it did the opposite. It trembled, and then seethed. The tendrils of mist turned to billowing exhalations, and vapor rose in a sudden fog. This had never happened before. Not that Brand's father had ever told him, nor that any rumor of legend whispered.

Brand waited. But for what, he did not know.

2. Will You Serve the Land?

A feeling came over Brand, and it was one that he had experienced before. But at all other times it was vague and slight, a hint of things that could be.

Now, it washed over him as a mighty wave. It was awesome, and it was a wonder. It was both joy and terror. For it seemed that his mind opened and expanded, or else a veil had been withdrawn that had dimmed his perceptions. He stood where he did, and he gazed upon the churning water of the Ferstellenpund, but at the same time he had a sense of other lands and other places. Deep into the earth his mind plumbed, and it also streaked high into the thin airs above the earth. North, south, east and west it sped also. And it seemed to him that he heard whispers of joy and far-off wailing, as though the land itself spoke to him of what was happening to the people who dwelt upon it.

The water of the pond began to still again, but now there was a presence in it. He saw nothing, but he felt it. And the sense of awe that overwhelmed him before redoubled now. The others fell back behind him, but slowly, reverently, Brand knelt upon the stony shore.

He looked into the water, and there was a face there. Human it appeared, but he could not be sure. Nor could he tell age, for the face was ageless, and in her eyes, for it was the face of a lady, it seemed to him that all the woe of the ages was caught, but also all the joy. Wise was her gaze, and tranquil, yet behind it lay an indomitable will, stronger and more enduring than mountains.

And the lady spoke, her voice clear but coming from no one place. Rather, it seemed as though the woods about him spoke, and the very air thrummed with her voice.

"Hail, Brand. Do not be alarmed. No harm can come to you here."

Brand remained kneeling. "This I know, Lady, for you are the land itself, and ever have I striven to protect the life to which you give rise."

She smiled at him. And it seemed that sunlight bathed the dark woods.

"Yes, you have done this. And I thank you. Yet I must now ask more. Will you devote your life to me? Will you serve the land?"

"I will, Lady."

Her smile deepened, and it was like sunlight on a winter's day. Brand gazed into her eyes. They seemed at times brown, and hazel and then green. They were wells into which a man could fall forever.

"I have watched you, Brand. I have felt you move across the earth. Your deeds are great, and your fame grows. All over the land I hear rumor of your name."

"Fame is fleeting, Lady. This you know better than I."

"You are powerful too."

"All power grows old and withers, Lady."

"You could be an emperor, for you could conquer realms and gather armies. The riches of kingdoms are yours for the taking. Who could stop you?"

"I stop myself, Lady. I have no desire for those things. The riches I truly seek are now forever beyond my reach."

The image within the water paused then. It could have been for a heartbeat, or for eons while the sun tracked the sky and the stars wheeled in oblivion. Brand did not know which, for he still gazed into her eyes and he knew that in this place time had no meaning.

"Then will you serve the land?"

"I will serve you."

"I am pleased. Take back your sword. You will have need of it, lòhren."

Brand knew what she had meant when she asked if he would serve. But this puzzled him.

"You call me lòhren, but lòhrens wield no sword. They carry rather a staff."

If it were possible, he would have thought her expression amused, though perhaps it was some shimmer of water that altered her face.

"You are not as other lòhrens. Your talisman is not a staff, but the sword. Take it."

It was then that he saw the rest of her body, for the water seemed to move and clear. She stood within it, upright, and in her hand she held the hilt of a sword. His sword that he had cast into the tarn broken.

She rose then, and all the while that she moved, still she fixed him with her gaze. Up, out of the water she ascended, and it trailed from her in streams and yet her skin was dry and so also the cloth of the simple white dress she wore. But the sword dripped water in her hand when she held it before him, now by the blade with her two hands, the hilt pointed at him.

He reached out, reverently. His right hand took the hilt. It felt good in his grip, but suddenly his sense of connection to the land strengthened even further. Something of her passed into him, for now both held the sword together and he felt one with her, one with the land.

And then her hands were off the blade. The world seemed dimmer, and for the first time Brand remembered he was in the woods, and the strange sounds of the forest came to life around him once more, reminding him of where he was and drawing him back to it, and back to the tasks he had yet to accomplish in this small, small part of the world.

"I will serve you well, Lady."

"This I know, Brand. And this I say to you. You will be like no lòhren that has gone before, for you will be a warrior, and a lòhren, and a king all. You will sire kings, and of your line will spring the hope of the north." She paused and her eyes glittered with thoughts beyond what Brand could discern. "Know also," she continued, "that the enemy comes. And with them, gods. It falls to you to defeat them."

Brand held her gaze. For her, he would risk his life. He had done so many times in fighting for the land.

"I am a mere man, but I will contend with them as best I can."

"This also, I do not doubt," she answered. "They will kill you if they can, but you are resourceful. And though they be gods, yet still they fear you. Let that give you courage and confidence. Your task is very hard. Perhaps your hardest yet. But you are Brand, and you do not die easily. You may yet prevail."

She reached out and touched his cheek gently, as though in blessing. Then she sank noiselessly into the water and was gone. The surface of the pond was still again, reflecting the purple-blue sky as it had earlier.

For a few moments Brand stayed kneeling. He did not trust himself to stand, such were the emotions that roared through him. A warrior, lòhren and king he would be. And of his line would spring the hope of the north. What did it all mean?

But he would get no more answers waiting here. What answers he would have would come fighting men. And gods. But only if he survived those battles. Yet the sword in his hand would help him, and he rejoiced that it was whole and his again. It did not matter how. The land had given it to him. It was both a sword and the symbol now of his stature as a lòhren. It was subtly changed, too.

He gripped the sword tightly and stood, turning to face the men he had brought. They remained kneeling, and were pale-faced and trembling. They looked at him with wide eyes, and he wondered if they would ever look at him the same again. Even Taingern and Shorty.

"Rise!" he commanded. "We have work to do."

3. The Tomb

The shadow of fear was upon Horta, and he did not like it.

How had things gone so wrong? Only he and Tanata had survived the wrath of the old Letharn spirit that Brand had somehow summoned or loosed upon the world. The rest of the Arnhaten were no more. The thought of it shamed him. But what followed had been even worse.

It was with disbelief that he had watched Brand fight Gormengil, and win. And in winning somehow sway the Callenor to join him. One moment they had been at war, and the next Brand led both tribes. *It was the breath of the dragon.* For the first time Horta understood exactly what that meant. Brand was touched by fate.

But so too was Horta. He had a task to complete. He had been chosen for it, for out of the countless searchers through years unmeasured, it was he who had found the tomb of Char-harash. It was he who would draw him back to life. And nothing could interfere with that now that he was so close. Not even defeat and the ruination of all his plans.

It still burned him like fire. He would never forget slipping away like a thief when Brand usurped control of the Callenor. He had found Tanata, taken horses and fled before they could be found and stopped.

For long years Horta had schooled himself to harden his heart. He had done things that would shrivel the soul of an ordinary man, but the shame of defeat had done something. Emotions flowed through him all the time now. Anger. Fear. Grief. He liked none of them, but stronger than they, and more welcome, was lust for revenge and the knowledge that it would come to pass. An army of Kar-ahn-hetep were on the way, and not even the combined forces of the Duthenor and Callenor could stop it. And when they conquered the land, the resurrection of Char-harash could begin. Then his own life could begin anew again also, for he would be the right hand of the god-king.

They rode down a steep bank. Tall pines grew to the left. To the right, the lights of a faraway village twinkled palely. Too close, Horta knew. Yet this was a populated land and even traveling at night there was a risk of being seen.

"Where do we go, master?"

Tanata had followed him loyally, never questioning him until now. But it was a good question, and it needed an answer.

"Where we must. Where our duty requires us to go. And where we will be safe from prying eyes."

In truth, Horta had not known where to go. It was only when the question had been asked that he understood the answer. Until then, he had just been getting away.

"Is anywhere safe for us now?"

"No, lad. Nowhere is safe. But some places are safer than others. We need the wilderness to hide us. And we have a place to guard until our army arrives. We go now to the tomb of the god-king."

Tanata accepted that news in silence. Although, perhaps he thought one place was as good as any other. Or perhaps he was still in shock from all that had happened. Horta would not blame him for that. He felt it himself. But his disciple had learned other things in the few nights of fleeing that at least Horta had known before. He had learned that the tomb of the god-king had been found, and that his time of resurrection approached. That had been as great a shock as anything Brand had done.

They slipped away into the dark. The slope was behind them, and the tall pines just a clump of darker shadows. Somewhere in the distance a dog barked, and Horta felt fear upon him.

He resisted the urge to gallop. The dog was far away, and no one would come to investigate. He might be on a farmer's field, but the Duthenor went seldom abroad at night. They preferred the warmth of their hearth fires, and the comforts of home. Things that Horta did not have, and anger replaced his fear.

He wondered again how it had come to this. His plans lay scattered. The men who followed him lay dead. The barking of a dog caused him fear. Nothing, it seemed, had gone right since last he had cast the Runes of Life and Death.

At least he had supplies. Enough to last a good while, and he would need them because there was nowhere he could go to buy any. He must disappear from sight until the army he waited on arrived.

So it went for the next several days. Traveling by night, and avoiding the habitations of men. Riding well clear of roads, and hugging the shadows like a thief. He liked none of it, but eventually they arrived at the tomb of the god-king one night in the gray hours before dawn.

Tanata deserved to see what he had risked so much for, so they dismounted and tethered their horses at the base of the hill. Together, they walked up the slope and then cleared away by hand the soil that Horta had left there to obscure the man-made stone of the tomb entrance.

Quickly, the cartouche of the great king was revealed. Three stars, one ascendant over the other two. They gleamed in the shadowy air, and Tanata trembled.

"That is enough for now," Horta said. "When our people arrive, the resurrection will begin."

He began to push dirt back to hide the stone once more, but the stars gleamed with sudden light. The earth trembled, and he lost his footing.

Even as he tried to stand, the earth groaned and roosting birds all around screamed into the night. Something was very wrong, and with a feeling of dread he began to understand.

4. Homecoming

Brand was at the fore of his army again. His Halathrin-wrought blade was sheathed in its old scabbard, and it felt good at his side once more. Better than ever.

Less welcome were the looks people gave him. Word of what had happened in the sacred woods was spreading. It could not be helped. But few now spoke to him, or looked at him as just a man. He had become more in their sight. He was a leader who spoke to the Lady of the Land, and one destined to contend with gods. No wonder they did not look at him straight. Even Shorty and Taingern seemed distant. With them, he knew it would pass. But the rest? He was not so sure.

The army marched down the High Way, and all about were lands that Brand knew well. This was where he had grown up. If the Duthgar was his home, then here was his home within a home. He knew every cottage, every copse, every stream and field.

Then came the moment he had yearned for nearly all his life, and yet also dreaded. The hall of his parents came into view. The hall of his ancestors into antiquity, and the seat of power within the Duthgar.

A road wound down to it from the hills on the other side, but the hall was also set on a hill, the highest for many miles around. The stone-crafted terrace before it was as he remembered. Up and down those stairs and platforms he had run and jumped as a child while his father's hall guards watched from their seats near the doorway above.

Brand's gaze turned to the hall. Proud it stood, the largest and fairest in the Duthgar. The broad gables were decorated, and the long-sloping roof designed to shed snow gave it the characteristic shape of any hall, even if bigger. The doors he could see too, huge slabs of oak bound by black iron.

But he would not pass through them, and the thought of that was grievous. He wanted to, but destiny, if there were such a thing, made no allowances for his wants and wishes.

The enemy was coming, and speed was critical. He must meet them before they came to the lands he loved. Not just the Duthgar, but all the tribes of the greater Duthenor people. He would not see the enemy ravish them. He would give them no opportunity to burn fields and homesteads. Nor to destroy villages while he waited and gathered more men. Those same men could come to him while he marched, and already riders had been sent ahead to give warning and to ask for help.

He thought that help would come. Though the tribes were different, once they had been closer. In times of war, before even they came to these parts of Alithoras, they had banded together under a war leader. They would do so again. They *must* do so again.

They drew level with the hall, and his gaze lingered on it. Would the chance ever come again to see it? He was not sure. The Lady of the Land had foretold he would be a king. But of whom? Of the combined Duthenor tribes? Perhaps. But she had also said that of his line would spring the hope of the north. What did that mean? And yet he had always yearned to explore the northern mountains of Alithoras. They drew him like a moth to light. But for any of that to happen, he must live. At the moment, that did not seem likely.

The hall passed from view. He set his gaze forward, and forced himself to think of the task at hand. He had not had the homecoming that he dreamed of, but he had something else. The sword of his forefathers was at his side. So too his friends, and an army at his back. And the memories of his youth would be with him all the days of his life.

The High Way soon began to take on a downward slope.

"What's ahead of us?" Taingern asked. "The land seems to be changing."

Brand was grateful for something to take his mind off things. He wondered if Taingern guessed that, and asked the question to distract him. He was always sensitive to other people's moods.

"The high plateau that runs through the Duthgar comes to an end here. Pretty much, the Duthgar ends with it. Beyond, and to the east, lie the lands of the Callenor."

"And what of the road?"

"It begins to deteriorate quickly from here. At least it used to, and I doubt that has changed."

"Does it still head southward?" Shorty asked.

"No. Soon, it'll turn south-west. It hugs the end border of Callenor lands, and of the tribes beyond them. Truly, it's not much of a road, but it must still have been traveled by the Letharn. Better to say really that those lands border it, for the road was built long before any of our people came here."

They walked their horses ahead. The going was easy, for the road was still good and the downward slope helped. But soon the way narrowed, and the road ran in half loops instead of a straight line. This was to find the least steep gradient and to help stop the road from eroding.

At each corner, the land below came into view. It was lush like the Duthgar, but flatter. Yet soon the expansive view disappeared. A great forest grew up, all of tall pines and shades of green mixed with shadows.

"You didn't mention *that*," Taingern said.

Brand knew what he was thinking. The way ahead was a good place for a trap or ambush. He did not believe the enemy was here yet, but he could not rule it out. And he trusted the Callenor, more or less. At least those with him, but he was entering their lands now, with an army, and he could not be sure of the reception he would receive.

"Time to send out scouts," he said.

"Time to proceed slowly," Shorty answered.

5. A Time of Change

Horta and Tanata fell back a little way down the slope. It seemed that the hill itself had buckled and moved.

"Earthquake!" Tanata yelled.

Horta wished that were true, but he knew it was not. Dread gripped him. Fear such as he had seldom felt stabbed at his chest, and his breath came in painful gulps. This was no earthquake. It was what he had striven to achieve, but it was too early, and he was not prepared. Nor did he understand how it was coming to pass without the proper rites and invocations of power.

"Stand back!" he yelled, but even though he did so, he never took his eyes from the flat stone of the tomb entrance.

The earth stilled. But the birds in the dark treetops continued to shriek. Then came a sudden booming, muffled by dirt and stone. It thrummed through the air and Horta felt it beneath his feet.

Three times that dreadful sound tolled, like a mighty bell beneath water. And on the third, fire darted from the cartouche and smoke rose, greasy and black.

The stone of the tomb entrance cracked, and then it fell into rubble. A dust cloud rose, and the air became choking, but neither Horta nor Tanata moved.

Before them lay a gaping hole in the side of the hill, and in the darkness of that pit something moved.

Horta knelt, and seeing that Tanata stood motionless and dazed, he grabbed him and pulled him to his knees.

"Kneel," he whispered, "and pray for your life. Glory is now ours, or death."

Out of the pit a figure emerged, and Horta slipped a norhanu leaf into his mouth and bit into it to release its powers. This was all wrong. It should not be happening. Not like this.

The figure clambered into view. Dirt covered it. A once-white burial shroud clung to it like a husk, and even above the smell of dust Horta caught the strong odor of oils, herbs and resins used in the preservation rites of the dead.

"O Great Lord!" he cried. "Your humble servant is here to aid you."

Horta bowed his head, even though he was kneeling, but still his gaze looked up. It was never wise to take your gaze off kings or gods.

Char-harash towered above him. In his right hand he hefted a mighty war hammer, blackened by the blood of ages past. His left was a claw of withered flesh.

The god-king looked down as though upon a beetle, deciding whether to ignore it or crush it beneath his feet. Or to use it for some menial purpose. Horta did not care for that look at all.

"I know you," rasped Char-harash. His voice was hollow, and it smelled of the tomb. "You have served me. Rise! Rise and live. You will walk in my shadow and serve me still in the days to come."

Horta stood. He beckoned with his hand for Tanata to do the same, for the god seemed to ignore his presence. Better to have company to face what was to come than to be alone.

"O Great Lord," Horta answered, and it was a sign of his shock that he could think of none of the ceremonial titles that he should use. "How have you risen from the dead? Your people come. An army marches to aid you. I, with my own hands would have performed the rite of resurrection. But you bestir yourself of your own will, without rite or ceremony or invocation. How is it possible?"

Char-harash fixed him with his hollow eye sockets. It seemed that there was a glimmer of light within their dark recesses, but Horta knew the eyes were removed during the embalming process. Yet still, that stare pinned him just the same.

"Am I not a god? Do not even fate and destiny learn to bow before me as the long years pass? These things are true, yet also the stars and planets shine upon me from the void. Even now, in their endless trek across the skies, they align and the powers that form and substance this world shift. Some forces wane. And others, myself and my brother and sister gods, wax. Our power begins to increase, and the world trembles!"

Char-harash flung out a skeletal arm, though still the bonds of muscle and tendon and ligament held it together. "See!" he cried, and his bony claw of a hand pointed. "There is Ossar the Great, and there shimmers Erhanu the Green, and brighter than them all shines blessed Murlek. These give me strength. These sustained me through the darkness, and they draw me into the light once more as their forces twine and spill down upon this world. As water they are to the parched throat. They are the blood in my veins and the beating heart in my chest."

Horta had heard those names before. Though the names had changed through the ages since last Char-harash had seen them. But he had no heart in his chest. That, and the rest of his internal organs were removed to stop his body rotting. Yet here he stood, and Horta feared him. If the god spoke, who was he to deny the truth of his words?

This much also Horta knew. There was power in the land, and there was power in the light that shone from the distant void. And well might it be that some change there had woken the ancient spells laid upon the corpse of the king who would be a god.

Char-harash was not done speaking though. He hefted his war hammer high. "Life begins to run through my body once more. Strength returns. And even as I wake from the long sleep, so too do my brothers and sisters stir. The light of the void and the breath of the dragon touches us, calls us, beckons us towards the destiny we have chosen for ourselves. The time of change is here, and all things are possible."

"All the gods grow in power?" Horta asked.

"All," answered the god-king. "The gateways of the universe open and close. But now, safety! I grow weary."

Even as he spoke the first rays of the dawn sun shone over the land, and Char-harash flinched as though they stung him. He seemed less like a god now, the more he could be seen. And evidently the clear light of day hurt him.

"Follow me, Great Lord," Horta asked. "I know a place of safety nearby."

"It must be a place of shadows!" hissed Char-harash.

"It is such a place, Great Lord."

Horta signaled Tanata to gather the horses, and when that was done they mounted. Almost he offered the god-king a horse to ride, but the horses were restless in his presence, shying away from him. For his part, Char-harash eyed them with disdain.

So Horta led the strange procession away, and they traveled in silence. This he liked, for it gave him time to think. Much had happened, and many things that he did not understand, at least fully.

He led them along a winding trail that climbed higher among the hills. Char-harash kept up with them, striding beside the horses, and he looked at everything he saw with arrogance. Or contempt. Truly, the gods, old or new, were

24

in some ways the same no matter their differences. And at heart, Horta was sick of them. They demanded so much, and gave so little in return. If he had his youth again, he would walk a different path down the ways of his life. He would abstain from magic and gods and plotting. He would stay in the desert lands that he loved. The wild lands where no man walked, for that was the place to live a life.

But his youth was spent, and his choices diminished. Now, all that was left to him were the ways of Horta the Magician.

6. The Witch

Brand led the army forward into the forest. Hruidgar headed the scouts, and he had sent men forth to investigate. They had not returned, but the army could not delay. At any rate, the men left signals that the hunter could see. The stem of a certain plant broken and bent one way or the other signaled safety or danger. There were others, but the hunter alone knew them. And so far, all was well.

But Brand went slowly anyway. He led, and he kept watch. He also kept one hand near his sword in case of threat. It was not wise for the general to ride before the army. He could fall if there was an ambush. He could be targeted by a bowman from far away. Certainly, he would be known as the leader by any eyes that watched secretly, because men came to him to report and left to carry out orders. Yet, balanced against this was the example he set the men. He was not afraid. And for the whole army to see, with him rode men of both the Duthenor and Callenor tribes. So too the few men from the Norvinor tribe that had joined him. It was a display of unity, and it would help bind the tribes together. Until recently, they had been at war.

"It's a gloomy place," Sighern muttered.

Brand glanced around. They had now entered the forest, but the road still descended, and at this point quite steeply.

"Gloomy, perhaps. And yet I like it all the same. The forest is a world to itself, and I like the feel of them. Better to me than a city, any day."

Hruidgar glanced at him. He did not speak himself, but if anyone knew what Brand meant, it was him.

Yet it *was* gloomy in this forest, and it was large enough to swallow an army. Or a hundred armies. That the men who followed were nervous also was evident. They did not speak much among themselves as they marched, and all that could be heard was the tread of thousands of booted feet.

Brand was confident though. If an enemy was ahead, the scouts would find them.

For some while they continued, slowly but surely. Then scouts began to return. They reported no enemy. This was good news, and the leadership group that rode with Brand was relieved. Yet somehow unease grew within him, and he did not know why.

It was possible that an attack, if it came, would not be with swords but with magic.

"Stay alert," he said. His mood infected the others. They saw no reason for it, but they had learned to trust his instincts. Their hands were never far from their sword hilts, and if their gazes lingered in shadowy patches of the woods before, they stared twice as hard now.

But nothing happened. The road dropped down further, seeming to plunge into the forest that it cut through. More scouts returned, easy in their manner and reporting nothing ill.

Brand led his horse, still holding to the practice of walking as his men must walk. They seemed to like it, and he thought of them now. Stretched out along the winding road and vulnerable. He was their leader, and everything he did influenced their lives. Even their deaths, for surely many, many would die. It was his task to see that the fewest of them paid that sacrifice as was possible.

Fate was not his to control, however. If there was such a thing. But he knew he would blame himself for the

27

smallest of mistakes, for any life lost that wasn't necessary, and perhaps even for those that were. Who was *he* to decide what was necessary and what was not? Yet someone had to, and he trusted himself more than any other to make those decisions.

And he trusted himself now. The sense of unease increased. He lifted high his hand in a clenched fist, and behind him the army came to a standstill. Nothing moved within the woods. All was silent. But he waited, and the silence deepened until the air grew heavy with it.

"What is it?" whispered Taingern in his ear.

Brand gave the only answer he could. "I don't know. But something comes."

He drew his sword then. The leadership group around him did the same. And the hiss of thousands of swords leaping from the scabbards of the soldiers echoed them like muted thunder.

And still, nothing happened.

The tension deepened, and Brand embraced it. The army was forgotten. The people around were forgotten. There was just him and the forest, and the sense of a presence within it. He knew then that the Lady of the Land had changed him in some manner, or woken something within him. He was not quite as he was. He *knew* there was something coming, even before it was there.

Ahead, on the road, a figure came into view. The darkness of the forest shrouded it, and it held its head down. But Brand perceived who it was.

"It is the witch from the swamp," he whispered.

Shorty peered ahead. "Last time we saw her it was some creature of the gods pretending to be her."

"This is her," Brand answered confidently. "At least, what she was."

Shorty gave him a strange look. "What does *that* mean?"

"You'll see."

The figure glided toward them, not seeming to walk but coming closer anyway. Brand knew she had no need to walk. She was not there at all.

She came to a stop before him. Slowly, she raised her head and studied him a moment. If her lank hair and bushy brows worried her, she gave no sign. But her eyes were less rheumy than they were, and the warts were gone.

"You will have learned now that my foretelling is true, lòhren."

Brand inclined his head. If she gave no greeting, nor would he. "I didn't doubt them, not really. But you also said we wouldn't meet again."

She cackled then, hoarse and throaty. But there was an edge of bitterness to it. "I did say that, didn't I? And yet here I am. But my foretelling is never wrong. Quite the mystery, isn't it?"

"Not really," Brand replied. "You lied. Or you are dead, and not really here at all except as a vision."

She looked at him sternly a moment. "Aye, you have the right of it. Not much slips past a lòhren, eh? But which is it?"

"You are dead, lady." Even as he spoke, he moved his hand through her image and it passed through unobstructed. Gasps came from behind him, but Brand ignored them.

"How rude!" she said.

Whether that referred to his calling her dead, or moving his hand through her image, Brand was not sure. But he had no time to play games.

"Why have you come, lady? What troubles your spirit?"

She stood taller then. Almost she looked him eye to eye, and her hair was less lank than it was, and her face younger. The spirit of a dead woman could appear however it wanted to, and apparently she was tired of looking like a crone.

"Well, I'm certainly dead. And I didn't think we'd ever meet again. I think that prophecy was close enough. The truth is, I should have helped you. Perhaps if I'd joined forces with you, I'd still be alive."

"Perhaps," Brand answered.

She stood even taller. "Too often I thought only of myself. I had reasons. But now. Well, now I will help you, just a little. It's all I can."

"Why?"

The witch grimaced. "Sooner hide a strange scent from a dog than hide the truth from a lòhren, as the saying goes. Well, if you want the truth, it's this. It's not for you. What I say now is for revenge. And if I get it, it'll be sweet."

Brand nodded. "That, I can believe. Nor do I spurn it. Speak, and I shall listen."

The witch seemed surprised at his ready acceptance, but she should not have been. Brand knew himself to be practical. He also knew he needed help.

"Three things I shall say," the witch replied after a pause. "I can do no more. First, this. Your enemy may yet be your friend. When despair grips you, hold tight to that thought."

Brand did not know what that meant. He had too many enemies, and none would ever be a friend. But still, he committed the foretelling to memory.

"Second," the witch continued. "The breath of the dragon blows across the land. All things become possible. Change comes, and change can be shaped. Make it yours. Seize opportunity from your enemies before they seize it from you."

Again, Brand did not know what to make of this. It was good advice though. Fortune favored the bold, and he knew it.

"Third," the witch stated, and her voice had grown strong and her visage that of what she must have been in youth. "Self-sacrifice is victory. Offer yourself up in order to grasp victory from defeat."

Brand considered her, and she returned his gaze silently.

"Good advice all, I'm sure. But how am I to use it?"

"Ask no more! I can say nothing else. But remember my words. They won't help you now. They won't help you in the future. That's not what foretelling is for. Hold onto hope, that is all. And you will see by the end."

Brand knew this was true. Her talent was real, but that did not mean she could tell him what to do and what not to do. Her words would not change anything, and would not really help. But perhaps they would shape his thoughts in those critical moments when the time came. Perhaps they might make a difference. It would be a fool who did not heed her.

He offered a slight bow. "Thank you, lady."

She swept a hand through her hair. It was luxurious now, and longer. Nor were her eyes as they were. They were sharp and bright, and they bored into his own as if that was the way she read the future.

"I have done what I can, small though it is. This time, truly, you will see me no more. Good luck. You'll need it."

Even as she spoke the image of her began to fade. He caught a faint whisper of her voice. *I come*, she said. But she was not speaking to him. In moments, she was gone.

All around, the forest seemed to grow a little lighter, and the calls of birds and the chirping of insects seemed suddenly loud.

"Did you make any sense of her foretelling?" Shorty asked.

Brand sighed. "Not a bit. But I wasn't meant to. As she said, it was to give me hope. And hope we have. The task at hand isn't doomed, else she would have said so. Victory is possible, though it will be difficult."

That was not quite what she said. He had put a more positive light on it, but it was still the gist of things.

He signaled the army forward, and the sound of swords being sheathed in scabbards was like a raspy rush of wind. Then, once more, the soldiers followed as he stepped ahead.

7. All the World is Yours

Horta came to the woods he was looking for. They were not large, but the growth of pines was thick and old. They cast deep shadows, and within their concealment the god-king would find respite from the sunlight that hurt him.

Char-harash shuddered when they entered the shadows. It was a strange sight. A dead man walking, or a god coming into his own. A being of great power, and yet one scared of sunlight, even hurt by it. Why should that be?

There were no answers to such questions, but Horta would ponder it anyway. That was the way to discover hidden truths.

"Just a little further," Horta said. Char-harash seemed ready to lie down where he was, but there was a better place ahead.

The god-king had grown weak. The war hammer seemed in danger of dropping from his hand, and the long strides that he had started with a little while ago were now a decrepit shuffle.

But they came very soon to the place that Horta sought. It was just below the highest part of the hill, yet still the tree-growth was thick. The god-king had the cover he wished, but there was a glade at the very top where Horta could go to study the lands about and see what was happening.

A spring seeped away from beneath a boulder, and it would supply them water, if they used it carefully.

Char-harash wandered a few paces off the dim trail, and there he lay down beside another boulder. It seemed that he slept, and Horta had no desire to disturb him.

In silence, he and Tanata established a camp. They tethered the horses nearby, and fed them a little of the oat supplies they had. Later, Tanata would take them to the clearing at the top of the hill to graze.

While Tanata replenished their water bags from the spring, Horta himself built a ring of stones around a slight depression, and there he gathered dry timber for a fire, which he lit. The timber would not smoke much, and what smoke was given off would be dispersed by the tree canopy above. No one was likely to discover them because of it, and he was tired of cold meals and a cheerless camp.

For the first time in a while, he felt a sense of relief. If Brand hunted him, the pursuers he sent would struggle to find him. This was not his land, but he was no novice at hiding his trail. Nor would they be discovered here by chance. It was an isolated spot, and farmers and hunters must come only rarely.

He allowed the sense of relief to wash over him as Tanata sat nearby. But then his glance fell to the sleeping god-king, and his heart was troubled again.

Tanata followed his gaze. "I did not know that gods slept. Do they?"

Horta shook his head slightly. It might have meant that they did not. Or that he did not know himself. It was the latter, but Tanata did not have to know that. It, too, was troubling. Was Char-harash a man, or a god? The legends said he would *become* a god. If so, what was he now? Was he even alive or was he dead? What were his powers? Would they grow? Surely they must, but then again he had shrugged off the sleep of death and risen from the tomb himself. That was power beyond any mere man or magician. Truly, the forces of the universe must be in flux and the god-king attuned by his own talents and the spells of his funeral rites to draw on them.

He talked a little while with Tanata, softly so as not to wake Char-harash, and then they too lay down near the fire and slept. The last few days had been tiring.

It seemed that Horta had just drifted off though, when the voice of the god-king rang through the camp.

"Wake!" commanded Char-harash. "Wake!"

Horta rose from the ground, his head turning and his eyes darting about seeking some enemy. But there was no one. Tanata staggered up as well, fear on his face and his eyes wild. Yet they were alone with Char-harash, though evidently the god-king had rested. For he had risen and stood over them, though he stayed clear of the fire and took turns staring at them as though they had done something wrong.

Char-harash, having got their attention, stepped away from them and the fire.

"I must know what transpires in the land," he said.

Horta gave a bow, or at least the suggestion of one. He was not best pleased, and still his heart hammered in his chest.

"I will tell you what—"

"That is not what I want. I would speak to a fellow god, and I shall summon one. Stay silent, but be ready to serve."

Horta bowed again. This time he did so more deeply. He had recovered, and it would not do to displease his new master. Death would come of that, swift and sure. He had no doubt about it.

Char-harash began to chant, and Horta understood the words. It was the rite of summoning, but here and there the phrases were different and the inflection altered. Horta had been taught by his masters, every one of them, that the words must be spoken exactly the same. He had learned that the words were said just as their ancestors said them long ago. But it was not true. Toward the end, the words became quite different indeed, and Horta wondered what else he had learned that was not correct.

Even so, he slipped a norhanu leaf in his mouth and began to suck upon it. That at least was sure knowledge. The leaf eased fear and gave strength. Both of which he might need. But his store was growing low, and that disturbed him. He would have to begin to eke it out until he could replenish his supply, but he had a feeling he would need more of it than he ever had before.

The gods appeared in fire, smoke and mist. Shemfal came first, bat-winged and terrible. Su-sarat followed, in her human form rather than serpentine. And last came one Horta had never summoned. But it was Jarch-elrah, human-bodied and jackal-headed. Black was the fur over his dog-like face, and his long ears twitched. He was the god of the grave, and rumor claimed him mad.

Horta sucked harder on the norhanu leaf. These were gods who hated each other, and the thought of summoning more than one at a time frightened him greatly.

"Hail, brothers and sister," intoned Char-harash. "We must speak and plan, for the hour is come foretold in antiquity."

But the gods did not look at him. Instead they studied each other with hooded eyes. Jarch-elrah barked, although Horta soon realized it was a laugh, if a mad one. Shemfal gazed at Su-sarat, and there was murder in his eyes. Su-sarat grinned at him, licking her lips as though testing the air with her tongue.

Horta knew the history between these two, and he groaned. But Char-harash looked sternly upon them.

He drew the army to a halt a quarter of a mile away from the gathered Callenor warriors. To go further was to invite battle. Now was a time for diplomacy. It was a time for words, not a show of arms.

Sighern felt nervous. He was not sure why. The Callenor warriors ahead were not a threat. There were too few of them. Yet it was an important moment. How they acted might determine, probably *would* determine, how the remaining Callenor warriors throughout the land acted. It was important that hostilities were avoided. It was even more important that every single warrior capable of fighting joined Brand's army and fought with him. How else could he have a chance of winning the great battle to come? How else could he hope to defeat gods, as the Lady of the Land said he must attempt to do?

At just that moment, Brand had called him over and he did not know why. Furthgil was already there, and it was plain that he would be sent to speak to his countrymen. What need had either of them for him?

"I have a job for you, Sighern."

"Name it, and I'll do it," he replied quickly.

Brand grinned. "You're always so quick to agree. I like that, but it could see you in trouble before the end."

"No man gets through life without trouble."

Brand sighed at that. "True enough. Hopefully there'll be none now. I want you to go over to the Callenor tribesmen," he gestured with his hand toward the warriors ahead. "You're my spokesman. Tell them I want their help. Tell them why. And answer any of their questions with honesty."

This was not what Sighern expected. Why on earth would Brand send *him*? He was barely old enough to fight as a warrior, though he had accounted himself well lately.

"As you wish."

Brand studied him. "You have no questions?"

Sighern shrugged. "Your instructions are clear enough. Do I go alone?"

"No. Furthgil will go with you. He'll represent the Callenor that have already joined my army. But you represent me."

"Very well." He glanced at the Callenor lord. "We might as well get going."

But Brand was not quite done. He went to his horse and retrieved the Raven Axe of the Callenor. "Take this with you."

Sighern took the weapon, and he felt the hard gaze of the Callenor lord upon him. He understood. It was a symbol of the Callenor, and it should not be in his hands. And yet it was Brand's now, and he had given it to him, at least for a little while. Furthgil would just have to accept that. The why of things did not matter, although Sighern would certainly try to figure it out. It seemed strange to him.

"Good luck," Brand said. "And remember. I need these men, and all the others like them. If they join me, the rest will more easily follow their example."

Sighern gave a bow. It was not something that he normally did, and Brand never encouraged it anyway. The Duthenor were free men, although it was said that men groveled to kings and lords in the cities far to the east such as Cardoroth.

He left then, Furthgil leading his horse by his side, until Sighern mounted his own. Then they nudged the horses forward toward the Callenor warriors.

Furthgil said nothing. The man seemed upset, and Sighern did not blame him. Possibly, the lord had more claim to the Raven Axe than any other. Certainly more than he did.

He hefted it in his hand. It was much lighter than it looked. A careful inspection revealed that the handle was not even wood. It was some sort of metal, strong but very light. It was hollow too. This was why it was so light, and there were slits in it. This was what caused the strange sounds when it was swung through the air. Ingenious.

They merely rode the horses toward the gathered warriors at a walk. Anything faster could give the wrong impression, and that might end badly. But it gave him time to think, too.

Why had Brand sent him? Why had he given him the axe? He could not be sure, but it seemed to him that a leader accrued authority by others doing his bidding. Had Brand gone over himself, it would have lowered his status. That much was easy enough to see. But anyone could carry out such a task, and most were better trained and more experienced than he was.

That was a line of thought that yielded something. Brand was not stupid. He knew all this better than he did himself. So, was there a benefit in sending someone over to accomplish the task who was young and inexperienced?

It took him a few moments, but then the answer became clear. Brand had picked him for exactly those reasons. He was young and inexperienced. He was no trained negotiator. The warriors he was going to talk to would know that instantly. They would discern quickly if he lied, exaggerated or tried to manipulate them. Not something he would have tried, but he also had Brand's only advice to go by. *Answer their questions with honesty.*

Sighern was a lesser figure than the warriors he would talk to. He posed no threat. He would tell them the truth, and he would be trusted more than anyone else. The warriors would believe what he said more than anyone else, even Furthgil. He was one of their own, but he was old and wise enough to lie without being caught. Brand might have given him inducement to do so, in gold or some other reward.

It made sense. The worst choice was the best, and Sighern's estimation of Brand went even higher than it was. But why give him the axe? Might that not cause animosity? The warriors would not like to see it in Duthenor hands.

For this also there would be a reason. It was just a matter of working it out. What would Brand achieve by it? No. That was the wrong way of thinking. It was not about Brand or the Duthenor. Everything was about the Callenor.

The Callenor warriors were clearly visible now, just a few hundred feet away. Soon, they would recognize the axe. What would they make of it?

One thing Sighern knew. It would not intimidate them. Not in his hands. Not when there was just he and Furthgil facing hundreds of them. That was surely not the purpose Brand had in mind. Was it intended to surprise them? Certainly it would. But was surprise an advantage? He did not think so. It would not achieve much.

There was no answer to the question. Giving him the axe served no purpose that he could see. But again, it was not about him, Brand or the Duthenor. It was all about the Callenor.

The warriors ahead would be surprised by it. And uncertain. They would not be able to decipher its meaning any better than he could.

He considered that. Uncertainty. It was a powerful mental state. It made people pause and think. It stopped them from rash actions. And more than that. It showed that Brand was *not* undecided. Rather the opposite. It showed that he knew what he was doing, and why, and all the more so because he was making decisions they did not understand themselves. As well, it showed that he was in complete control of not just the Duthenor but the Callenor with him.

Sighern grinned, and Furthgil gave him a strange look. But there was no time to explain what he thought now. Perhaps the other man already knew. Afterall, Brand had spoken to him first.

They drew their horses up, and dismounted before the line of warriors ahead of them. Sighern gazed at their faces. They were hard men. They were true warriors, and they carried themselves with that sort of casualness that could burst into deadly action in the blink of an eye.

Sighern admired that. Brand, Taingern and Shorty were like that as well, only more casual and more deadly. But he was used to it. He held it in the highest of esteem, but it did not scare him. These men would not attack him. It would be a cowardly act, and he knew just by looking at them that however violent they could be, it was controlled and directed only toward protecting themselves and their land.

He led his horse forward a few paces, holding the reins in one hand, while in the other he held the haft of the Raven Axe. He gripped it high, near the double-bladed head to indicate he had no intention of swinging it, but still the eyes of the warriors flickered between it and him, and their gazes were hard. They knew it for what it was.

Tension filled the air, and Sighern spoke first, before Furthgil who was both his elder and one of them.

"Hail, warriors. My name is Sighern, and I've come here at Brand's bidding to talk."

He was met with a wall of silence from all these men, but one stepped forward a pace and answered. He was, perhaps, a little older than the others. Certainly his armor and clothes were of a better quality. He was of the nobility and their leader.

"Hail, Sighern of the Duthenor. My name is Attar, and I lead this band. Hail also Furthgil, who once dwelt in Callenor lands."

Furthgil grimaced. "I know you, Attar. Why do you say that I once lived in Callenor lands instead of calling me a Callenor? Do you truly believe my allegiance has changed?"

Attar looked him in the eye. "You've been gone from us a long time. And you come here now, you and other men who once lived here, joined to a Duthenor army. What am I to make of that?"

"You know why your countrymen are here," Sighern said. "And why the Duthenor are as well. You'll have received messages. But if you doubt them, then speak to us. Ask questions. I'll hold nothing back, and answer you truly."

Attar studied him, surprised again that he took the lead over Furthgil.

"We've received the messages. Interpreting them is another matter."

"It makes sense to be cautious," Sighern replied. "I don't blame you. But now you have a chance for more than messages. I've been with Brand since first he returned to the Duthgar. I've seen everything with my own eyes. Where you have doubts, ask me and I'll tell you what I know. Truthfully."

The other man seemed thoughtful. It threw him that Sighern was in charge, and that Furthgil did nothing to try to change that. But he showed little of this on his face, even if a glimmer of uncertainty gleamed in his eyes. But it too was quickly suppressed, and he asked an unexpected question. Sighern was prepared to talk of gods and foreign armies, but Attar appeared to have other concerns, or at least was not yet willing to go direct to the heart of the matter.

"What's Brand like? What sort of man is he?"

Sighern was not sure how to answer that. "What can I say? He's like no other man I've ever met. There's no one braver than he is. Time and again he's risked his life for his people. I don't think there's anything he wouldn't do for them. And the rumor is that he could have been king of Cardoroth had he wanted. But he kept his word and stayed regent only. He returned to the Duthgar, when he could have been a king, or lived like a king. That says it all."

Attar pursed his lips. "So, Brand would die for his people, you think?"

Sighern didn't hesitate. "He would. I believe that."

The Callenor warrior nodded. "And what of you? Would you in turn die for Brand?"

Again, it was not the sort of question Sighern expected. But he answered it truthfully.

"No one knows for sure what they're made of until they're tested. But yes, I think I would. At the least, I hope I have the courage for that."

Furthgil looked at him, then at Attar. "The boy has courage. Whatever else you doubt, don't doubt that. He and one other accompanied Brand and walked into our camp to speak with Gormengil. Three surrounded by thousands. That took guts."

Attar raised an eyebrow. "Guts indeed. I don't doubt it." He turned his gaze on Sighern again. "Tell me of this army that supposedly comes against us."

"We know it's coming. We don't quite know where or when, but it'll be near here and soon."

"And who is this army made up of? What do they want?"

"They're the Kirsch. They want to conquer the Duthgar and wake … I'm not sure. A long-dead king of theirs who is buried somewhere in the Duthgar.

49

Supposedly he'll be a god, and he'll conquer the world if he isn't stopped."

"And you believe these myths? For surely that's what they are."

Sighern held himself tall. "If someone had just told me, perhaps I wouldn't. But I've seen one of the gods of the Kirsch. She was real enough to me."

"I saw her also," Furthgil stated. "And sorcery besides. The times are changing, and the world shifts. There's danger in every action, but the greatest danger is to do nothing and hope things pass us by."

Attar looked at them long and hard. Then he glanced at the leaders of his men. What passed between them, Sighern could not tell. None of them spoke, but they still seemed to have arrived at a decision, or supported what decision they knew Attar had made.

He turned to Sighern. "Then we will join Brand and fight."

Sighern slowly raised the Raven Axe. "I expected nothing else. You're Callenor."

9. A New Banner

Brand was pleased with what Sighern had done. Hundreds of Callenor warriors had joined his army, and Attar now rode in the leadership group. He was a minor lord, but he looked a hard man, and used to fighting. More importantly, he sent his own messengers out. Word of his joining Brand would spread. It would convince more to do the same.

The army pressed forward. A sense of urgency descended, and though Brand did not know where the enemy was or how close, he felt that soon the scouts would bring him word.

They moved across the edge of Callenor lands. It became flatter still, most unlike the Duthgar, and the turf-roofed houses became bigger. This was a more prosperous area, and Brand could see why.

There were many fields, and they were quite large. But each grew a good crop of some kind of cereal. Oats dominated in the Duthgar, but here it seemed to be wheat. The grain heads were filling, but harvest was still some way off.

Almost it seemed peaceful. The late summer sun shone warm and hot, but autumn was at hand. The fields rippled to every breeze, the grain heads nodding. It was drawing on to harvest time, a period of hard work and then celebration. There would be many barn dances, and beer would be drunk while sausages were made and hung from kitchen ceilings to smoke. It was a defiance of the hard winter to come. But this winter would be harder.

War was coming. Blood would be spilled and lives lost. Men who should reap wheat and thrash grain would instead cut and stab at an enemy. Women who should sing harvest songs would weep. And many would die, perhaps all, if he failed.

He must not fail. The land needed him, and he served her. It was a pity that all his skills related to war, and the fighting of men in groups and single combat. Even magic was a weapon, though only against sorcery. But a man learned what life forced him to learn, and he acted according to the deeds that were required.

There was more to fighting though than the cut of a sword, and more to leading warriors into battle than being the best fighter among them.

He glanced at Sighern. He had asked the young man to keep the Raven Axe a little longer when he had returned and offered it back. No one was quite sure what to make of that, least of all the lad. Perhaps Taingern knew, for he was a deep thinker and he missed nothing, least of all what was hidden from plain sight. But no one else.

"Sighern," Brand said. "Do you still wish to be my banner bearer?"

The young man nodded enthusiastically. "Of course." The banner was not on display now though. Brand had ordered it taken down when they entered the lands of the Callenor. It was his birthright, and he was proud of it, but it would be provocative to them.

"Then I have something for you. Keep the old one in your saddle bag for the moment, but for now, use this instead. I've had it specially made these last few days."

He dug into his own saddle bag and handed the banner he had designed and ordered made to Sighern.

"Attach this to the old staff, and carry it proudly."

The young man withdrew the staff from a leather loop attached to his saddle, and he tied the new banner to its end by the cloth strips attached to it.

But it was only when he held it higher that it properly unfurled, and the design upon it became visible. The cloth gave a white background, and on the banner's bottom left was embroidered a red dragon, the emblem of Duthenor chieftains. But on the top right corner was the black raven claw of the Callenor tribe.

There was silence as Sighern held it high, but the young man merely glanced at it, giving a small nod of approval after a few moments of consideration.

"Of course," he said, almost to himself. "We're no longer just the Duthenor. This army is of Duthenor and Callenor warriors combined. Neither takes precedence over the other. This is a banner all can fight beneath, and die if they must."

Attar responded solemnly. "You are right."

Brand gave no answer. Yet again, the young man impressed him. His insight and understanding of situations and events was greater than could be expected from someone his age. Shorty and Taingern knew of the new banner, and they approved. But they had no sense of patriotism to either tribe. Their loyalty was to him.

It had been different with the Duthenor warriors he had found to make the banner itself. He had located men within the army who had some skill at sewing and embroidery, if mostly with thin leather for decorative saddles, reins and the like. When he had told them of the design he wished, they had resented it and even argued. Brand guessed that most of the Duthenor felt that way, but he knew it would change.

Sighern understood better. When the fighting began, warriors would not care much if it was a Duthenor or a Callenor beside them. All they would want was that their comrade held the line with them, fighting shoulder to shoulder and helping to protect one another. They would be one army then, and one people.

The army halted for a rest soon after. The leadership group wandered to the shade of an apple orchard by the road. The fruit was not ripe yet, but the skins of the apples were beginning to show color. The shade was good though, and it was a relief from the late summer heat.

But though he enjoyed the shade, Brand had work yet to do. He called over Bruidiger, the leader of that handful of Norvinor tribesmen who had joined his army.

10. Like Whey from Curds

Wena led his army forward, and pride filled him. The days of blood and glory were coming again. He was a magician and a battle leader, and the gods would favor him for his diverse skills.

Dust rose behind the troops, but not as much as previously. The dry lands of his home were behind him. The new green lands lay all about. Fat, luxuriant and soft.

Even what dust rose in these green lands would be less now. A cold rain had begun to fall. It was little more than a shower, but it would dampen the earth and settle the telltale haze. If there were any enemy eyes in this wilderness, it would help hide the passage of his soldiers. Other than that, he hated the rain.

He hated the land more though. So green and lush, and the wind always blew. It was late summer, but it seemed cool to him. How then would it be in winter? The thought chilled him. Snow and ice and razor-sharp winds, according to legend. The prospect of campaigning for years in such a place did not appeal. But the thought of the bloodshed to come warmed his heart. He would show Char-harash what he was made of.

Horta was a concern though. The man was soft. He had a reputation for treating his Arnhaten well, rather than as the slaves they were until they had endured years of hard service and learned the craft of the magician properly. A state few achieved. But worse, he was the discoverer of the foretold one's tomb. That would lift him high in the eyes of Char-harash.

And Horta would use that. Oh yes, he would use that. He would seek dominion of all the Kar-ahn-hetep eventually, but certainly in the first instance the army that came now to free and serve the god-king. That could not be allowed.

Wena grinned to himself as he marched. He would not confront Horta, nor challenge him for authority. He would greet the other man as a brother, and when opportunity arose, he would slip a knife into his back. That was how situations like this were handled. But Horta was powerful, very powerful indeed, so it must be done carefully.

Despite the weather, he was in a rare good mood. His mind flitted back to earlier this morning. He had ridden in one of the war chariots. It was an exhilarating experience, but not one that he ever had much opportunity for. The chariots were few in number, only some five hundred in total. And they were instruments of war, reserved for highly trained specialists. One driver and one warrior to each. Only they and kings were allowed to use them, and there had not been a king for a long, long time. That might change.

The savages ahead of them would not know proper military tactics, still less the means to face horse-drawn chariots that moved at speed and broke enemy formations. No, they would be surprised at that, and they would fall back in dismay.

The battle to come did not disturb Wena. He grinned to himself as he walked, but between one pace and the next that grin was gone.

Something was coming. The hair on the back of his neck prickled as it did when he performed the rite to summon a god. Only he had done no such thing.

He signaled the army to a stop, and drew his short sword. Was this some attack by the enemy? He felt magic at work, and that was always disturbing.

But it felt familiar also. It could not be the enemy. Unless it was Horta? Could he be launching a preemptive attack? It was possible, but he did not think so. He would need all the help he could get for the Rite of Resurrection that must yet be performed.

Smoke writhed up from the ground as though the earth itself was afire. Fire seethed in the air, and mist twined through it, turning instantly to vapor.

Three figures sprang into being, and Wena stumbled backward a few paces. Then he knelt. For he knew who these figures were. Shemfal, Su-sarat and Jarch-elrah. They were gods, and not just gods but leaders among gods. Nor was that alone what intimidated him.

It was unprecedented for three gods to appear at once. It had not happened in living memory. Perhaps not even in legend, but he could hardly think.

A shadow fell over him, and he knew Shemfal had stepped closer. His great wings moved and shimmered, and a terrible light was in his eyes.

"Stand, mortal," the god said. "If you have no courage, we will find another in this army to lead."

Wena rose. His legs were unsteady, and his heart pounded in his chest. Death filled the air, or at least the possibility of it, but he forced himself to look into the eyes of the Lord of the Underworld.

Shemfal gazed at him the way a man might study the fruit of a tree to see if it was ready to be picked.

"That is better," the god intoned. "If you would serve, you must have courage and wit."

Wena did not hesitate. "I have both, O Great One. Command, and I shall obey." He gave a small gesture to his Arnhaten, and they stumbled toward him. A sacrifice may be called for, and he had no intention of facing that request alone. Dying was for lesser servants, but the gods did not always know that. Better to have all his options close to hand.

Jarch-elrah gazed at him, as though reading his very thought, and those eyes pieced him for there was madness in them.

But it was Su-sarat who spoke. "Courage will be needed more than wit. We know your task, and we have deigned to help you. Our thoughts will be your thoughts, and you will have little need of your own."

Wena was not sure what that meant, exactly. But it revealed one thing at least that he liked. They did not intend to kill him. That was what mattered above all else.

It was time to try to take some initiative. "We hasten across the lands, O Great Ones. This Duthgar that we seek is getting close, according to my guide. Soon we will unleash war, and find the tomb of the god yet to be. Then—"

Shemfal towered over him, but as he stepped closer Wena observed the famous limp.

"We know this, mortal. You will do these things or die. But there is more you must do."

Su-sarat leaned forward now. "Peace, Wena. We have felt your tread on the earth, and the gods know you for a man of distinction. You are marked for greatness, and truly the days to come will allow you to shine. But there is more for you to accomplish in this fight with Brand."

She reached forth with her hand and touched his cheek then. The thrill of it ran through him.

"O Hunter of the Night, I am your servant. Command, and I obey. My guide has brought word of this Brand who leads the enemy. I will crush him for you."

Su-sarat smiled at him, and her gaze was kinder than the shade of an *uzlakah* tree in the desert.

58

"You will crush his army, but for that man ... I have a plan of my own. Leave him to me, but as for the battle with his forces, this is what you will do."

She bent near him, and her soft breath was upon his cheek. Just as well to remember that she was the Trickster, and honeyed words could swiftly become a venomous bite. But as she spoke, he liked the strategy that she outlined.

"First, travel swiftly," she advised, "for Brand himself hastens. Keep your main army with you, and make no attempt to hide. His scouts will find you quickly enough. But pick a man of judgement, and let him take a smaller army, one of three thousand men, and task him with flanking Brand in secret. This will not be easy. Let him have your best scouts in order to kill Brand's. Tell him also that failure is certain death, for should Brand become aware of him too early, his small army will be destroyed before you arrive."

Wena nodded slowly. He would not interrupt, for he liked the plan, and he knew what was coming next.

"When you approach Brand's army," she continued, "slow down your advance. Give the second army time to maneuver, for it must needs travel wide and further than yours to escape detection. Then when you have joined battle, the second army will descend upon Brand's in surprise and fury. Caught between two forces, the enemy will be destroyed."

It was as Wena thought. But he was not so sure of the outcome.

"Yet still the enemy may retreat," he said. "If so, and if well led, they may salvage the situation and surprise will be lost."

"And what will you do then?" Su-sarat's voice was a whisper.

59

"Then I shall follow with speed and force, harassing him all the way. He must turn and fight, else be destroyed piecemeal. But in the end, by force, or surprise, in one hour or over days, he *will* be destroyed."

Su-sarat nodded. "Let it be so, but you will find that he does not retreat. Be wary that he does not attack just when defeat is likely. He is that sort of man."

Wena noted that. He was surprised that there almost seemed to be admiration in the voice of the goddess. But likely he imagined it. The gods did not admire men.

Su-sarat withdrew, for Shemfal loomed closer. Wena felt the enmity between them, and it seemed they did little to try to hide it. She sneered at him, and he pretended that she was not even there, assuming a lofty arrogance befitting a lord among gods.

Jarch-elrah growled deep in his throat, but after a moment Wena interpreted that to be a laugh. It sent a shiver down his spine, but he ignored it. His attention was on Shemfal only.

"The Duthenor are soft," the Lord of the Underworld declared. "When the time is right, slaughter them in blood and fury. It would please me. And all the better will those who remain alive come to serve their new masters."

Wena bowed, and when he looked up again the shadow of the god had passed from him, and Shemfal and the other two had their backs to him, walking away. In a moment, they disappeared in roiling smoke. But the limp of the bat-winged god had been obvious.

One of the Arnhaten nearby laughed nervously. "The legends of the feud between the snake and the bat are true," he said. "And the snake had the victory."

Wena did not hesitate. In a single motion he drew his sword and decapitated the man. The head rolled on the dirt, and the body stood a moment, blood gushing. Then it fell in a heap.

Wena casually bent and cleaned the blood off his blade with the man's cloak. Then he stood.

"Bury the man," he ordered the other Arnhaten. "Make it a narrow hole, and place the head in first with the body after, feet up."

Wena moved aside and issued orders for the detachment of the second army. He would squeeze the blood from these soft northerners like whey from curds.

11. He Would be a King

Bruidiger came over to Brand, as requested. His every step was casual poise, and he had the look about him of a warrior born. The grace of a dancer was needed to be a swordsman, and a will of iron harder than any blade. This man had both. But it was more than a look, for Brand had seen him fight. Even so, the man smiled now with good nature. The Norvinor, Brand had discovered, were a happy and laughing people, quick to joke and quick to make light of themselves. It was a trait Brand admired, and all the more so in deadly warriors.

"Can I do something?" Bruidiger asked.

"Yes. I have a job for you, if you're willing," Brand answered.

"Name it, and it will be done."

"You're like Sighern – always agreeing to things before you know what they are."

"Guilty as charged, my lord. But then again, I can always try to back out of things afterward if I don't like them."

"True enough," Brand said. "But I don't think you'll want to back out of this. We need more warriors, and your homeland is on the further side of the Callenor lands. It's getting closer. So, would you be willing to go to your chieftain, and to tell him what's happening? And then, on my behalf, ask him for help?"

"Of course," Bruidiger replied. "But I can't guarantee what he'll say. But if rumor of events in the Duthgar has already reached him, it'll help."

"I can ask no more than that you try."

"When do you want me to go?"

"Now. I'll have a fast horse given to you. And one for each man in your small band if you like. They may prefer to go with you."

"I don't think so. Their place is here, even if I'm not with them. What comes is a threat to us all. But I'll ask them."

It was not long after that Bruidiger sped away on a black mare. It was a fine horse, though not as good as Brand's roan. Just as well that Bruidiger's men had not gone with him – the army had few horses and fewer still that could keep up with the black.

Brand turned his thoughts away from Bruidiger. He would succeed in convincing his chieftain to send warriors, or he would not. There was nothing more Brand could do about it. But his own army was a different matter.

For all that he was trying to create a sense of unity among the two tribes, it was not easy. The lords of either tribe seemed to bicker among themselves, and they were quick to feel slighted at an accidental word. To be sure, there was mistrust there, but it was more than that, and Brand knew it.

They all sought power. It was what lords did. And the current situation created a void. For the moment, all power came from Brand. He was careful to assign tasks, responsibilities and praise equally, but he also made choices based on merit. It was a concept they did not understand. They had come to power through networks and connections and the luck of being born to certain parents.

They knew though that war was at hand, and battle and death. If he himself was killed, a likely enough possibility, someone would have to take charge. Most of them wanted it to be themselves, and they fought for power now to make their rise easier in such an event.

A few of them had also seen what he had long known. The new banner had made it clear, for those with the eyes to see. The Duthenor and Callenor had once been a single people. They could be so again. They could become powerful, and have a powerful king to lead them.

Brand knew he could do that. But should he? The Lady of the Land had said he would be a king, but not of whom. And always the mountains of the north beckoned him. Why was that? And how did it fit into anything?

The army was on the move again, but Brand found an opportunity to talk to his oldest and most trusted friends, without others listening in.

"Should we win the battle ahead," he asked, "what future do you see for the two tribes?"

Shorty scratched his head. "You always like to plan ahead. Me? I'm only thinking about the fight just in front of us and how to win it."

Brand laughed. "Pretend all you like, Shorty. But you see things as clearly as the finest strategist, and you're as wise as any philosopher."

The other man grunted. "If you say so. But alright, this is what I see. You're already forging the two tribes into one nation. And you know as well as I that if we win the battle ahead, these men who have fought together will draw close as brothers. Suffering together does that. You'll have them all in the palm of your hand, and a kingship beside, if you want it. And if you're alive."

Brand thought on that. Shorty had said it bluntly, as he always did. But his insights were correct. He wondered how long Shorty had seen his plan to unite the tribes into one kingdom. Probably from the beginning.

"What do *you* think?" he asked Taingern.

His other friend answered quietly. "The kingship is yours, if you want it. But you don't. The Duthgar was your home, but it isn't any more. More than you ever dreamed of is within your grasp, but it has been before, and you left it behind. You have another destiny. But you also have a problem. Only you can unite the tribes. The lords quarrel among themselves for precedence, and without you, hostility will break out. Who else is there that can unite them all?"

Brand knew that was truly the question. There was no one. But then again, he had given thought to it before. Nothing was impossible, and he had a few ideas. But Shorty was right. They had to win the battle ahead first. When that was done, *if* it was, then things would be clearer.

His musings were interrupted though. Hruidgar, that strange hunter he had made head of the scouts, approached.

"What news?" Brand asked.

"Nothing. To the south my men report empty wilderness, as expected. So too the south-west. To the north, well, we don't go too far because they're Callenor lands. But we've seen no forces there, hostile or friendly."

"The Callenor will join us I think, but just as the Duthenor in the Duthgar it will be smaller groups at a time. Keep the scouting up there, because I don't want any surprises, but I don't fear they'll attack us." He swept his hand out to the south-west. "Out there is the true enemy. Somewhere. They're coming for us. Time to send the scouts further afield, I think."

Hruidgar nodded and ambled away. He never was one to speak much, but he knew what he was about when it came to organizing the men he had picked and been given charge of.

The army went ahead. The land changed again, and northward rose in a series of sweeping slopes. They were not steep, and they caught the sunlight. Here established vineyard after vineyard, and the place was famous even in the Duthgar. This was the origin of the wine the Duthenor drank. They had a taste for it, even if they preferred beer and mead more.

The vineyards were not as grand as what Brand had seen in Cardoroth, nor of the same quality. But with time and attention, they could be.

It was rumored the people here were prosperous, for they profited well off the expensive wine. But profit or not, they had a good life and it was said their autumn harvest festivals were the best in the lands all around.

Not for the first time, Brand wished he made a simple living like that. For all his power, they lived the better life.

12. The Old Masters

Horta had rested through much of the day, for the flight from Gormengil's army, or the army that had become Brand's depending on how he looked at it, had been wearying in the extreme.

It was night now, but only just. He felt fresher than he had for days, and though the exhaustion of physical effort had fallen away, the mental strain of fear of pursuit had not left him. But it was reduced. He and Tanata had taken turns through the day to climb to the open glade at the crest of the hill and observe the countryside for miles all about. There had been no sign of any search.

Dusk had just given way to full night. Tanata had woken too, and he threw more wood on the fire. It was time to cook some dinner. This was a chore for the acolyte, but in truth Tanata had proven a surprisingly good cook. Even with the limited supplies he had to work with, he turned out edible meals. And he liked doing so. How unusual that someone who was learning the great mysteries of the universe should also like the mundane.

But Tanata had proven a surprise in so many ways. Not least his acceptance of their new situation, and his seeming lack of anxiety. The man was confident, although part of it was an act. His brethren had been killed around him. He now served a dead man, not quite come back to life, who would yet become a god. He took it all in his stride, as the Duthenor would put it. But there were shadows under his eyes and he whimpered in his sleep without knowing. The fear was there, but masked to near perfection. It was an admirable trait.

In the shadows, Char-harash woke and stirred. The god seemed to stumble upright, and then he strode over.

"Food," he said, his voice harsh and dry. "I must have food."

"We have supplies, O Great One. Tanata will prepare something."

The god-king seemed to consider that, then he shook his head. To Horta, it seemed the gesture was filled with frustration.

"I need more than you have. Stay by the fire, and do not go out into the dark."

Char-harash ignored them then, and he moved away into the night and disappeared from sight.

Horta felt the eyes of Tanata upon him, and he knew the unspoken question in the other man's gaze, but he ignored it.

"Prepare something for us," he said, turning his own gaze back toward the shadow-haunted forest.

Tanata did not answer. He merely went about his task quietly and efficiently, but Horta, despite not answering the unspoken question, could not ignore it in his own secret thoughts.

He put more timber on the fire, leaving a section of embers alone so that Tanata could use it to heat their cooking pot. It was a night for a large fire, but he could not risk making it any larger than it was for fear of being seen, however unlikely that was.

Unwillingly, his thoughts turned to Char-harash. Could he not eat normal food? Would it not sustain him? That seemed to be the case, else he would have eaten in the camp. But why go out into the dark? Had he need of living flesh to eat? Would he hunt some beast and eat it raw, thereby increasing his life force?

A still-beating heart, and the blood pumping from it, of a sacrifice was part of the Rite of Resurrection. It was said to help bring the dead back to life. But there was great magic involved in that rite also, and he had always taken the blood to be symbolic rather than necessary. Yet he could be wrong. It was possible Char-harash, having exited the tomb by himself, now undertook what was necessary to sustain himself in his own way.

But no magic had been invoked at the tomb, at least that Horta had sensed. That must still be to come. Or, possibly, the god-king had worked his own spells and used the influence of the heavenly forces to fortify himself before anyone arrived.

Anything was possible, and Horta did not like not knowing the answers. Was Char-harash alive in any true sense of the word? Could he really become a god? And if so, what kind of god would he be? If he needed to feast on living flesh now, would that always be so?

Horta had no answers, and he ate the food Tanata prepared in a melancholy silence. The answers to all his questions would come, eventually. But still, the urge to use the Runes of Life and Death pulled at him now. If ever there was a time for foretelling, this was it.

They finished eating, and Tanata cleaned up. The night wore on about them, and Char-harash did not return. But it seemed that the dark was alive with unseen eyes all about them.

Horta made up his mind. "I shall cast the runes," he said to Tanata.

The young man merely nodded. He had expected it. Perhaps it was what he would have done, or maybe he had come to know his master well. Whatever the case, Horta was pleased, and glad that at least one of his acolytes still lived. Serving a god by himself would be a lonesome task.

Horta moved a little way from where he sat so that he did not look directly into the fire. He motioned Tanata to join him, and allowed him to sit level with him rather than behind. It was not something that his masters had ever done with him, but the times were changing, and the old ways were not always the best.

He began to chant, and his words flitted up into the night the way that smoke and sparks from the fire rose in a swirling plume.

Forces gathered around him. Dark forces fit for summoning only at night. He felt their presence disturb the natural air. He could not see them, but much of magic was like that. The unseen was the most powerful.

And despite not seeing them, he could still put names to them. All his masters that had gone before him, and no few of his enemies as he had risen through the ranks of magician society. Ten there were, and they came now at his summons to do his bidding and reveal the future, as they were constrained to do.

But with their presence they also brought hatred. Enmity thrummed through the magic that bound them. He felt them strain against it.

He continued to chant, his voice louder now and the strength of his will greater. Each word he uttered with perfect clarity. Last time he had cast the runes, there had been some mistake. He would make none now.

Certain that all was well, he exclaimed the last words of the invocation in a commanding voice. Then he sat in silence. A moment he hesitated, for fear came upon him every time he was about to cast the runes. Knowing the future was a dangerous business.

He did not pause long though. This was a task that he did not like, but one that he had performed many times. He knew the pattern of it, and the ceremony that had come down of old. None among the Kar-ahn-hetep knew it better than he.

He slid his hands into the pouch that contained the runes. They were cold to touch, which disturbed him.

70

Normally that was not so. They were fashioned of bone, not metal.

It did not matter. He would cast them and read the future, whatever it was. The wise man looked forward to nothing, and the wise man feared nothing. What would be would be.

He shook the bones in the pouch ten times, as ritual demanded. This was to ensure the caster could not choose certain runes deliberately.

His fingers seemed numb from the cold now, but he took hold of the bones that he felt and withdrew them from the pouch.

All around him the spirits of the dead flew, but they were hushed and invisible, nothing more than a whisper of pressure somewhere on his mind.

Then he cast the runes, flinging them to the ground as he always did, careful to let them fall where they would and not try to guide them in any way. But no sooner had he done so than a great tumult broke out.

The spirits screeched through the air, and the flame of the fire dipped and wavered. Even Tanata gasped, and Horta glanced at him quickly. The man was pale as snow.

Horta did not understand what was happening. It was then that he saw the runes, and the blood drained from his own face. The spirits raged all about him, but he was heedless of their presence. He had eyes for the runes only.

He studied them. The finger bones of dead men lay there, and nothing in all the world mattered save them. He counted them. And then he counted them again. There were ten, and there was no mistake.

A cold fear settled into the marrow of his bones. His heart thrummed, and his mouth worked silently. He had no words to express his dismay.

Ten bones. It signified one thing, and one thing only. Catastrophe of the highest order. The ten bones must *never* be cast at once. Never. And if they were, which legend recorded only perhaps once before, it meant, death, destruction and calamity. Had the sky fallen upon him in a ruin of shattered stars he would not have been more surprised.

But he was Horta, a magician of power. Let fate be what it would be, he would face it with courage. He stood up slowly, drawing Tanata with him, and guided him to stand further back.

Then he drew powder from one of his many pouches, and cast it at the bones. Fire flared and sparked to life, flashing brilliant white in the dark, making the campfire seem pale. Twice more he did so, uttering words of power.

Smoke rose, dark and acrid, and the very earth seemed to melt and roil. The bones were destroyed, what they revealed blotted from his sight, and the spirits of the dead that the runes entrapped were loosed. No more would they be constrained to serve him, and their faces billowed up in the smoke and leered at him.

Then, with cries of glee, the images of the old masters faded away on the night. The fire died, but tendrils of smoke still rose from the blackened patch of ground. Horta watched them, silently.

He felt a hand on his shoulder. "Come away, master."

With slow steps, Tanata led him to the other side of the campfire, and then he urged him to sit down and rest. When he had done so, the acolyte fetched him a cup of water.

"Drink, master. All will be well."

It was a lie, and they both knew it, but it was well meant.

Horta sipped from the cup. The water tasted like ashes in his mouth, for that was what his life had become. Catastrophe was coming, and he would be at the center of it. But what shape would it take?

Something of his old spirit returned. If catastrophe was to be his lot, so be it. He would still make the most of it. The true man endured disasters and came out the other side. This is what he would do, no matter what.

He straightened, and took another drink of water. Then he looked at Tanata.

"We will not speak of this again. Erase it from your mind. Banish it from your thoughts."

"Yes, master," Tanata replied. But Horta saw from the look in his eyes that he would never be able to do so. He knew the meaning of ten runes all at once, just as well as Horta himself did. And what man could foreknow coming disaster, and ignore it?

They sat in silence after that, sheltering close to the fire. Horta built it up into a blaze, for it was a night where warmth and light were needed. He would take the risk of being seen by any of the Duthenor that searched for him.

In truth though, he did not fear the Duthenor. Had Brand sent men after him, they would have found him by now. Or else they searched, but had found no trail to follow. And if they had not found one in the first few days, then they would not find one now.

Whatever disaster was to come, Horta did not think it had anything to do with the Duthenor. It would come from the gods.

Even as he thought that, Char-harash moved stealthily from the shadows and entered the camp. He sniffed at the air, as though he smelled the unnatural fire that had burned here.

He seemed to dismiss it from his mind though. With a glance at his two servants, but not a word of greeting, he strode over to the other side of the camp where he had slept before and lay down.

Horta exchanged a glance with Tanata, and he saw that the other man had observed the same thing he had.

Char-harash was stronger than he had been when he left.

Horta should have been happy with that knowledge. The coming of the god had been all that he had striven to achieve for years. But instead, he wished only for the tranquility of the desert wastes. All the more so, because he feared he would never experience it again.

13. Nothing is Destined

The vineyards became larger as Brand led the army forward along the road. They covered the slopes, and the neat rows of vines continued for mile after mile. But eventually, they came to an end.

The land changed soon after, and steep hills rose all about. The road turned and twisted, climbing the steepest, and at its top were ruins.

"Those are *old*," Shorty said.

It was true. Brand noted the collapsed walls and piles of rubble. The stone itself seemed weathered, its surfaces roughened by wind and rain and cracked by frost.

"It was here before the Callenor ever came to these lands," Furthgil advised them. "We stay away from them, but there's no rumor of ghosts as with Pennling Palace."

The reference to Pennling Palace was apt, and Brand guessed this building was constructed by the Letharn too. It was not so large, or grand, but from what remained of it there was no doubt it was a fortification too. And one that was perhaps older, when the Letharn border stretched deeper into foreign lands.

They kept going, for Brand knew that haste would serve him well. It always had in the past. Travel quicker than the enemy expects, was his motto. It was advice given to him by his father, but he had also studied it in the records of the great campaigns of Cardoroth, and other nations whose wars were recorded in Cardoroth's libraries.

Give the impression of the expected but execute the unexpected, was his other favorite motto. This too had been used to great success in many campaigns, but for the moment at least, he saw no way to implement the tactic. The Kirsch were coming, and he was going to meet them before they had a chance to ravish the Duthgar or its allies. It was a simple strategy, and its best chance of success was to bring battle to the enemy before they anticipated it.

But for all that speed was necessary, he raised his fist and halted the progress of the army as he had done at the coming of the witch.

But this was no witch. Now, he felt the presence of a god. Su-sarat was nearby, even if she had not revealed herself yet.

How Brand knew this, he was not sure. But his instincts were sharper since he had met the Lady of the Land, and he trusted them.

A fine mist rose from the ground before him, and it formed into the image of Tinwellen, the guise the goddess had used to trick him in the Duthgar.

After a moment, she stood there, dark hair gleaming and eyes smoldering, but she was not alone. Gormengil stood next to her. He had once been a chieftain. He had once been a man. But he was something more now, or less. He gazed at Brand with dead eyes that did not blink, nor was there any expression on his face.

Su-sarat spoke, and her voice was high and clear.

"We meet once more, Brand of the Duthenor. Have you brought all these men to worship me, as you should? Have you come to worship me yourself?"

"Neither," Brand answered. "We have come for battle and victory."

The goddess laughed, and the sound of it was a joy to hear.

"I speak of love, Brand. And you speak of violence. Is there a future for humanity if that is your true nature?"

Brand grinned. "Pretty words. And from a pretty lady. But they disguise reality, and I have better things to do than bandy words with a trickster."

Her eyes smoldered even more, and there was a sudden anger in them, cold and sharp.

"Pretty? Is that the best compliment you can give me? I suppose you would call the ocean a mere drop of water?"

She turned slightly to face Gormengil. "What do you say, my lord?"

The man who had been Gormengil immediately knelt on one knee before her.

"O Goddess, you are fairer than the sun, and I bask in your glory. When you look away from me, the cold of winter grips my heart. When you gaze into my eyes, I am a drowned man who wishes only to plunge deeper."

Gormengil did not move, except that he swung his head to look up at Brand. "Shall I kill him for you, O Goddess? Speak the words, and I will fulfill them."

Brand held the gaze of his former enemy. There was no emotion there, no spark of life. He *had* been his enemy. But now he was like a dead man, moving to the unseen strings of his mistress like a puppet.

"Not yet, my pet," Su-sarat said to him, bending slightly to lay a hand on his head as a woman patted a dog.

Brand sensed Furthgil tremble beside him. Gormengil had once been his lord. He was thought to have been dead, but he was not. Su-sarat had somehow saved him, but in that saving he had been changed. His body lived, but his *mind* was dead. Yet still, he had been the chieftain of the Callenor, however briefly. Would they want him back again?

But Furthgil made no move and spoke no words. He saw who Gormengil served now, and what he had become.

"What do you want here?" Brand asked the goddess. "Time presses, and I have better things to do."

The way he spoke was an insult. It was intended to be. How she reacted would reveal more of her character.

But she merely smiled, and her eyes sparkled. "Oh Brand, how I would have enjoyed breaking you to my will. But no matter. The past is the past. And in remembrance of the good times we shared together, I shall give you this warning."

She gestured for Gormengil to stand, and he rose smoothly at her touch, but she did not take her gaze off Brand.

"Leave these lands," she said, lifting her chin and speaking proudly. "Gods conspire against you, and you cannot challenge our might. Leave warfare behind you. Leave bloodshed behind you. I know you better than you know yourself. You are no warlord, nor heartless warmaker. Each drop of blood spilled is as a tear in your eye. This I know, and thus I give you opportunity to prevent it, and a chance to forestall guilt that will weigh down your very soul. Brand, leave all this behind, and go wherever else your heart takes you. But do not stay here."

The goddess spoke with power, and even Brand felt the force of her words. All eyes turned to him in expectation. Many seemed worried and anxious, for if he left there was no hope to fight off the Kirsch.

"Lady," Brand answered. "I hear your words. Even, I would say, they are well meant. But if you truly knew me, you would know that the guilt of betraying my people would weigh me down more than all else. With a clear mind and a patriotic heart, I answer you. And not just for the Duthenor, but all the tribes threatened by your coming. I will not go. Rather, I bring us all together in defiance of your army and your magic, and even of your gods. Shall I defy it all? If I must."

78

A deep silence fell, and no answer Su-sarat gave. Instead, she bowed her head as one in deep thought, or perhaps sorrow.

"So be it," she said at length. "I have given warning, and you have given answer. I can do no more for you, and truly, I regret your passing."

"I have not passed yet, my lady."

"But you will, and the world will mourn you for a while. As will I."

"Don't mourn me yet, goddess. I'm a hard man to kill."

"And yet, you are just a man, if a powerful one. You possess a warrior's skill, and a king's bold heart. Even, you possess the magic of a lòhren. But these things will avail you nothing. Change sweeps over the land. The starry void spins and turns, and the gods come again. You cannot prevent it. You can only fall before it. Even the mountains topple when the ocean rises in fury. It is destiny."

Brand laughed. "Destiny? You are wrong. Nothing is destined. Nothing is fixed. You and your kind have a chance to return, and I have a chance to stop you. That is all. And I *shall* stop you."

Su-sarat sighed. "Such courage. You could be one of us, but you never will be."

"I do not wish to be."

"Then there is nothing left to say. We will not meet again."

Slowly the image of the goddess turned to mist. Brand watched, wary to the end for she was the Trickster. But she spoke no more, nor made any attack.

Gormengil was another matter though. His body was vague, shifting vapors disappearing in the air, but his face was still clear. And he spoke, his voice void of emotion, but somehow still filled with a cold desire.

79

"You will not meet her again. But you *will* meet me. Dread that day, for it will bring ruin to your army and spill your blood upon the earth even as mine was spilled."

Then the Goddess and Gormengil were gone, but a chill remained in the air.

14. Only by Chance

Hruidgar was sick of the army. Too many people, and too much noise and talk disturbed him. He was a loner, and did not really like people at all. But Brand was different. When he spoke, it was to a purpose. And where he led, others followed.

But for all that Brand spoke seldom, his gaze was never far away, and those eyes seemed knowing. It was not possible for him to *know*, and yet there it was. As uncanny a thing as Hruidgar had ever experienced.

Few remembered the days of his youth. He was older than he seemed. But once, he had left the Duthgar. Three years he had been gone, and when he returned men questioned him where he had been, and he refused to answer. That had given him a reputation, and afterward he was avoided.

That was for the best. And for his part, he became a hunter, roaming the wilds and bringing meat into villages in harsh winters and furs for trade at other times. He had never grown rich, but he had avoided people as much as they avoided him.

They were dead now, most of them. Few knew his name, still less that he had ever been away from the Duthgar.

But he had. And it was the best time of his life. Seeking adventure, and to forget a girl who had spurned him, he joined a merchant caravan heading south. He had wanted to go to Cardoroth, but the merchant was going to Esgallien.

One destination was as good as any to him though. And anyway, it had not been the destination that mattered. It was always about the journey, and the strange lands and wild places of Alithoras that lured him. That merchant had a knowing gaze as well. He was a man who understood.

So it was that Hruidgar fell in with men in Esgallien who understood him too. The *Raithlin* they called themselves, a last offshoot of a legendary scouting organization. Their skills were extraordinary, and their courage just as great. They taught him, and he trained with them. Even, he undertook missions with them. But he never became one of them.

Learning what he could, reveling in their skills, he formed a camaraderie with them that he had never felt elsewhere. But eventually the call of his own homeland came to him again.

He returned home. And if he was a loner before then, he was more so afterward. But Brand had drawn him out, given him authority and responsibility. He recognized his skills, but he had no way of knowing how they were acquired. Yet still, those blue eyes fixed him at times as though they saw all secrets.

Hruidgar would serve that man well. It was almost a vow. Seldom had he contributed to his community. You could not contribute to something you were never really a part of. But Brand had picked him out and trusted him with a task. He headed the army's scouts, even if there were not enough of them and he was sick of all the people and noise.

But he *did* contribute now. At the same time, he knew his own character. He needed time in the wild by himself. The scouts would report directly to Brand for a while, and all would be well. He would return refreshed and ready for the last stage of the great events he had been caught up in.

He rode a slick black mare, though he would have preferred to be on foot. It was easier to scout that way, and to remain unseen, but he was getting older now, and the horse would allow him to cover much more ground.

But where should he go? He had sent scouts out in all directions, but most had been sent to the south-west. Only a few had gone south, so he turned his mount in that direction. Those men needed his help more than the others. There were fewer of them, and they were the less skilled. In truth, all the scouts were no more than hunters. They were crafty in the wild, but had they known the true skills of the Raithlin they would have been in awe.

He nudged his mount down a slight slope, and once more checked that his assortment of throwing knives, daggers, short sword and bow were all in place. A man could never be too careful, but there would be nothing to find where he went. Still, old habits died hard.

He slipped away into the night, and it welcomed him like a long-missed friend. The army camp was perhaps a half mile away now, but it was invisible. The noise of it, a low rumble in the distance pierced by high-pitched shouts and laughter, still came to his ears though. But soon that would fade. So too the scent of smoke in the air. And when they were gone, he would be truly alone.

He moved south, a shadow in the night. Not only was he leaving the army behind, but the populated edge of Callenor lands. Ahead was the wild. There were no farms and fields. Even hunters would be scarce. He eased forward at a walk, letting his mount choose a path and keeping his own senses alert to the surrounding dark.

He was alone now, and he began to think like himself once more. Almost, he was like another animal that roamed the land. He scented the air. He lingered on the higher points of ridges, looking further afield to see if there were campfires in the darkness ahead. He never moved too far along a straight line, because he had no wish to be predicable.

But even here in the wild, he would not be quite alone. Some few of his men had been sent this way too. They would be out there, somewhere. Though he doubted they would see him or he them.

Brand had allowed him quite a few men. More than he would have thought, but it was still not enough. Maybe that was just as well. It gave him reason to leave the camp and have a look at things for himself. It would only be for a day or two, but that would be enough for him to regain a sense of his own self. When that was done, he could return to the bustle of the army and the milling together of all those men.

The night drew on. He rested at times, even dozing a little now and then. At other times, he led his mount by hand. He did it where the ground was rough and he feared the mare might make too much noise or break a leg. Brand did it all the time, and he had no such reason, though still a practical one. He did it to show he was one of the men. If he walked where they walked, he would fight where they fought. Warriors respected that. A single gesture such as that was worth a thousand words.

Dawn began to break. It was a quiet time, that period where night gave grudgingly way to day. It was a dangerous time too, for a man's thoughts could drift and ebb, and the tiredness of a long night could catch up with him.

That was particularly dangerous for a scout. That was when an enemy would spring a trap. Not that there were any here, yet still it seemed just that little bit too quiet.

Hruidgar sat taller in the saddle. Just thinking of enemies gave him the sense that he was being watched. The wilderness always did that, but the man who ignored his instincts in the wild might soon be dead. And those instincts sparked to life now. Even the mare seemed a little uneasy, flaring her nostrils nervously as if catching the scent of something that she did not like.

He rode on, but warily. Even so, it was only by chance that he discovered the body.

15. Not my Heritage

The army was on the move again, and the scouts had brought in word of a great gathering of warriors ahead. Five thousand strong it was, but it was a Callenor force and not the enemy.

The Callenor had gathered more quickly than Brand had thought. It was a good thing, yet it still made him nervous.

The two forces drew closer, and out of the Callenor a small group detached and came to Brand. They would be lords, and their gazes swept over the bigger army, but came back to rest again and again on the banner that Sighern carried.

Brand gave the reins of his horse to Taingern, and stepped forward to meet them.

"We've come to join you," one of them, a silver-haired man, said simply.

"You're welcome, and you're needed," Brand replied.

They shook hands and greeted one another. But their gazes kept going to the banner. Brand said nothing, waiting for them. And one of them at last mentioned it.

"What does the banner mean? I've not seen its like before."

"It means this. The Duthenor and the Callenor fight together. For a time, we'll be one army with one purpose under one leader."

The silver-haired lord spoke. Hathulf, Brand had learned he was called.

"For how long a time?"

"Until the threat we face is beaten. And after? Only as long as you wish. I'll not forge a kingdom by force. I'll not make the Duthenor and Callenor one people. Not unless they want it."

The older man seemed thoughtful. "And what if they *do* want it?"

"Then all things are possible. But let's not ride the horse until it's caught and saddled. We have an enemy to beat first. Nothing else matters until that's taken care of. Nothing at all."

Hathulf seemed to accept that. But his gaze, when it was not on the banner, was on the Raven Axe that Sighern now carried through a loop in his belt.

"And what of that?" he asked, gesturing toward it but not naming it. "Why does a boy carry it and not you?"

Brand was not sure if Sighern appreciated being called a boy anymore, but no insult was intended and the words seemed to roll off him.

"I don't carry it because it's not my heritage." Brand said no more, but he waited. Another question would follow soon after.

Hathulf grunted. "According to the messages I received, you won it and it's yours. So too the chieftainship of the Callenor. At least according to ancient law. But if you don't want the axe, why not give it to a Callenor lord? Why not give it to someone whose heritage it belongs to?"

There it was. And it was a dangerous question in its way.

"The axe is temptation," Brand answered. "It's mine by right, but if I give it to a Callenor lord, what then? Would he not begin to wonder, holding that axe, if he could unite the Callenor beneath him? Would not the thought arise in his heart that he could be a chieftain? And what then of our alliance?"

"So, you mistrust us then?"

Brand replied swiftly. "I trust my understanding of the hearts of warriors and lords. Tell me. If I gave you this thing, would you carry it and not be tempted?"

Hathulf grinned at him. "You've been honest with me, so I'll be honest with you. I'd be tempted. Very tempted indeed. So I agree. Best that it shouldn't be in my hands, nor any other lord of the Callenor. Yet still, why give it to a boy and not one of your great warriors? I see men with you who seem no stranger to the press of battle."

"I give it to Sighern because he also, despite his youth, is no stranger to the press of battle. He has the courage of a true warrior, and wits as sharp as a well-kept sword. But most of all, I give it to him because he's young. He thinks little about the Duthenor and the Callenor, and all about fighting and beating our enemy. I can trust him with it. To him, it's an implement of war rather than a symbol of leadership."

The eyes of the Callenor warrior studied Sighern anew, and silence fell.

At length, Hathulf spoke, and it was to Sighern. "High praise indeed. But now that I look at you properly, the words ring true. Sighern I'll call you, and boy no longer."

Sighern answered him. "Too high praise I think, for I'm just a simple farm lad. But I'll swing this axe in the battle to come, and I'll fight for the Duthgar because that's where I was born, and I'll fight for the Callenor because I have the great honor of carrying this axe for them. I'll do my best to be worthy of those who wielded it before me."

Hathulf nodded slowly. "I believe it. Though not all who held that axe before you were men of honor. But most were, and I don't think they'd be displeased for you to carry it now."

He turned again to Brand. "I'll serve you, and my men with me. Lead us well, for if the messages are true, you'll need to be the greatest war leader our peoples have ever known."

"Sadly," Brand answered, "that's exactly what I am."

16. A Long Night

The light was a little stronger, for the sun was close to breaking over the rim of the world, and Hruidgar could see better.

And he did not like what he saw. Scattered around were the prints of wolves or wild dogs. They had spent time here, for their spoor was everywhere. But most of all, they had gathered at the base of an oak tree, ancient and hollowed in its lower trunk. Save there was no opening. This had been blocked by a mighty branch fallen several years ago.

It all looked natural, but he knew it was not. That branch, large as it was, had been moved.

Carefully, Hruidgar dismounted and tied his reins to a sapling. He studied the branch, and one side was paler than the other, and the darker side showed signs of dry rot. Until recently, it had lain on the ground.

No animal moved a branch that size. Still less to place it against the opening of a hollow tree trunk. Men had done that. Hunters maybe. But a cold twist in his gut told him that was not the case.

Something lay hidden in the hollow, and he guessed what. It must be a body, and the effort of concealing it was for one purpose. It was not meant to be discovered.

Had it been left in the open, crows would gather. They would draw any scout in the vicinity like moths to the flame, and whoever had done this did not want that.

Hruidgar spat. Theories, he knew. They were worth nothing. He must have the facts, and that meant pulling aside the branch. He had to know, for if the enemy scouts were here, then the army was not far away, and Brand would be flanked and surprised.

He took a grip of the branch and heaved. It moved with difficulty for oak was heavy, and it was near as thick as his body.

With a grunt, he let it fall. A faint smell of decomposition met his nostrils. And he forced himself to look inside the hollow. He knew what he would see, but he had to confirm it.

Inside was a corpse. Ants covered it, and glazed eyes stared up unseeing. Eyes that he knew. Durnheld, a hunter the army had picked up after the battle with Gormengil.

Hruidgar cursed under his breath. The dead man was little more than a youth, all eager for adventure. He had skill and talent, but he was also young and inexperienced. Hruidgar had sent him to scout out here to protect him. Better this than where the army was expected.

How wrong he had been. The man's throat had been cut, and dried blood showed on his tunic where he had been stabbed at least once. He had been killed, and then his body hidden.

Why?

Murder, perhaps. Anything was possible. But he knew in his heart it was an act of war. Durnheld had been killed by enemy scouts. And that meant one thing. The enemy was close. Two things, actually, and Hruidgar cursed again. The enemy was close, and Brand did not know.

But what should he do now? Seek confirmation, or return to Brand swiftly and give warning?

It was not an easy problem to solve. But first things first. Regretfully, he must hide the body again. Durnheld would get no decent burial. There was no time for that, and without putting the branch back up wild animals would devour his corpse.

Hruidgar muttered a few words, long forgotten he had thought them, but they were the Raithlin funeral creed, and they came unbidden to him now.

Well did you serve and protect
High was your honor, low your hate
Your love for good was a beacon of light.

Then he reached out and pulled the man's cloak up over his head. There would be no funeral shroud for him. No mourners and no ceremony. The hollow of a tree would serve as his tomb. But at least he would rest for eternity in the wild lands that he loved.

Hruidgar heaved the branch back into place, and then he turned and leaned his back against it, thinking hard.

Durnheld had not been dead that long. If enemy scouts had done this, then how far away were they? He could not know, but they might still be close. Close enough that they may have seen his coming and followed him. They could, even now, be stalking close and setting him up for a kill.

He studied the landscape around him. He saw nothing out of place, but nor would he. Durnheld was young, but he did have skill. To kill him, the enemy scouts must be good. Perhaps very good.

His gaze fell to the ground close by. The tracks that he had seen were from dogs rather than wolves. The middle toes of dogs were slightly larger, whereas the four front toes of wolves were the same size. The bare ground beneath the massive oak was soft from years of falling leaves, and the sun was now fully up. The dog tracks were quite clear, but he spotted more marks that he had not seen before.

There were no human tracks, except for his own. But there were signs of disturbance, nonetheless. A leafy branch had been used to smooth over the surface. This had removed all trace of the people that had been here, but it left its own tell-tale signs. Whoever had done this was taking no chances.

It was not reassuring. It spoke of skill and determination. Neither of which he wanted in abundance in an enemy. Nor did it make his choice of what to do any easier. Should he return now and warn Brand? Or should he discover the enemy and learn their numbers?

It was the first that he wanted to do. He was never very brave. And as much as he hated large groups of people, the army offered safety, of a sort. At least until battle was joined. Moreover, Brand needed to be told that the enemy may be flanking him.

But really, what good would that news do him? Was the entire Kirsch army here? Had it split into two? Was this only a small expeditionary force? These were all things that Brand would need to know. If he did not, he would be forced to send out more scouts to discover that information, and more young men like Durnheld would be killed.

No. He wanted to go back, but he must go forward. He must find the enemy, tally their numbers and discern their intention. That was his job as a scout. That was the job of a Raithlin.

He spotted a fallen branch, and used its leaves to hide his own boot marks. If the enemy scouts returned, and they might do on purpose to see if anyone had discovered what they had done, they would not know their presence had been revealed. But they would certainly know that he was here, for he could not hide his horse's tracks.

There was nothing he could do about that. His presence alone was reason enough for them to try to kill him, but if they knew he was aware of them there would be a greater sense of urgency. Far greater.

He rested the branch down on the ground when he was done, trying to make it look like it had fallen there naturally. Then he turned and surveyed the scene. It was just as it was when he discovered it, and he could do no more than that.

Next, he turned his gaze to his backtrail. A long while he studied it, seeking any signs that he was being followed. He saw nothing. But that did not mean much. A good scout, or even a group of them, would not allow himself to be seen.

Still, there were no other indications either. Bird calls were one thing he listened for, and so too the sight of birds rising up from trees which might indicate something moving below them. But there was nothing like that.

Yet the thought would not leave him that someone was there, and perhaps more than one. Instinct? Fear? He was not sure, but there was nothing else to do but get on with his job.

He loosed the reins of his horse from where they were tied, and mounted swiftly. If need be, he could gallop now and cover a lot of ground, but that was the last thing he would do. Only an attack would bring that on. Otherwise, it was best to move slowly and carefully. In that way, he might escape detection. But the horse would make it harder.

He knew he left tracks, and he could not hide them. But he moved ahead, being careful to change direction often so that he took no predictable path. He avoided good places for ambush too, and tried to keep himself from being highlighted on open ground on a rise.

Everything he did was designed to avoid being found, but deep in his heart he knew the enemy were out there, and they were good. He had sufficient skill to avoid them, but that alone was never enough. He needed a touch of luck too.

So he moved through the day, and though he saw nothing out of place nor heard anything out of order, his anxiety only grew.

The land about him began to change. There were less pines and more oaks. It flattened too. This was, perhaps, an advantage. Without high points that would serve as lookouts, he would be harder to see from a distance.

If he had the opportunity, he would have hidden during the day and traveled only at night. That would have been safer, but there was no chance for that. Time pressed, and the sooner he found out what was happening, the sooner he could return to Brand and give him an opportunity to develop a counter strategy.

Brand was a canny man, and a war leader the like of which the Duthgar had never known. He snatched victory from the hands of defeat, again and again. What was to come though, that would be a greater test than all that had gone before. All the more reason that he *must* have accurate knowledge of what the enemy was doing. Without it, he was doomed.

Hruidgar guided his black mare down a slope at an angle. And when he was halfway down, he changed direction. This sort of maneuvering was costing him time, but being predictable could cost him his life.

To the west, the sun sank low on the horizon and shot the scattered clouds through with pinks and reds. The oak trees, scattered across the land like the clouds scattered in the sky, cast long shadows.

Night was coming, and he breathed a sigh of relief. He had not liked traveling through the day, but it had been necessary. Now, he would travel through the night. It would be safer. But it would be a long night without rest. He was too old for this kind of work, but there was no one else to do it for him. If one of his scouts had been killed, likely enough the others had too. Durnheld was the best that he had sent out this way.

He reached the bottom of the slope, and angled south again through a small cluster of trees. The light was fading fast now, but even so he saw the track in the grass.

It was a boot mark, and it was fresh. Very, very fresh. Even as he watched, he saw a blade of grass within it spring upright again. It was only minutes old. Perhaps not even that.

17. Ambush

Hruidgar knew he was a dead man. Only chance had taken him at this angle down the slope, but it had caught his enemy by surprise. Had he not come this way, he would never have known the danger.

But knowing the danger did not necessarily help him. Not much at any rate. If more than one scout was stalking him, he certainly was dead. But, perhaps he had a chance if there was only one of them.

He lifted his gaze off the boot mark. It was best just now not to give away any indication that he knew the man was somewhere close by. If he did so, the scout would be twice as wary. If he thought that he remained undetected though … that would make him complacent. Hopefully.

It was a chance Hruidgar had to take. He had no others.

He moved ahead slowly, letting the horse pick its own way forward. The option was there to kick his heels in and gallop. That might swiftly take him away from danger. Or straight into an ambush.

No. It was best to continue just as he was, and to allow himself an opportunity to see the ambush that would be sprung on him rather than gallop blindly into it.

Dusk was covering the land in a shadowy blanket, but there was still enough light to see by. If an ambush was coming, it would likely be soon. No scout would want to try tracking him in the dark. It would be hard to do except by staying close, and at night that meant a much higher chance of stepping on a branch in the dark that would give away his presence.

No. He would be ambushed, and it would happen very, very soon.

He moved ahead slowly, trying as hard as possible to show no sign of anxiety. All the odds were in favor of his enemy, but at least one thing might work to his benefit. The enemy would expect him to be surprised when the attack came, but if he was ready for it, he just might be able to turn that surprise around by acting quickly.

Another thing was advantageous too. Durnheld had not been killed by arrows but by blades. It seemed the enemy scouts carried no bows, and that was a stroke of good fortune. Had they done so, he likely would already be dead.

He tried to determine where the ambush would be laid. He had seen where the enemy scout had been, so he put himself in the man's position and tried to work out where he would go.

There was lower ground ahead and to the right. A man could lie there unseen, and then rise and attack with sword or knife when his target came closer. It was a possibility.

But ahead and to the left was a clump of straggly trees. That too was a good hiding spot. But which would it be?

His life depended on guessing correctly, for he could not guard well against both sides at once. And things would be even worse if there was more than one enemy.

He made his choice. Had it been him, he would have avoided the lower ground to the right. The grass was taller there, and the chances of leaving a visible trail were higher. The clump of trees to the left offered shorter grass that would leave no trail, and also the chance to remain standing behind a tree rather than lie down. This would mean a quicker attack when it was time to act.

Hruidgar let out a slow breath. He wished with everything he had that he dared to string his bow and notch an arrow, but then his element of surprise at not being surprised would be lost.

He licked his lips. An irrational urge to laugh came over him, for the idea of surprising someone by not being surprised suddenly seemed ludicrous. But on such a situation his life now turned.

He could not string his bow, but he did have throwing knives up the sleeves of both arms. Surreptitiously, he let the one on his right inner forearm slide out of its sheath and into his hand. That would enable him to throw better to the left. But if he was wrong, and the attack came from the right, he would be disadvantaged. He wished he could feel the hilt of a knife in each hand, but he had to control the horse, and when the attack came that might be needed for the horse would surely shy at sudden movement.

He drew close to both likely ambush places. His heart raced, but nothing happened. Had he been wrong about them? Was the man somewhere else?

He had nearly gone past the places when a man rose suddenly from the grass on the lower ground to the right. Hruidgar had chosen badly, and yet had his knife been in his left hand he would now have to try to turn back and throw, which would be too slow. As it was, he was able to fling the knife in his right hand in a quick backhand motion.

But the other man was throwing too. Hruidgar dropped low in the saddle, and the horse leaped forward in surprise. One of those things saved his life.

He did not even hear the noise of the passing knife. It must have missed him by a good amount, but his own had struck home. The man, fully behind him now, reeled backward.

Hruidgar pulled hard on the reins, turned his horse around, and kicked in his heels. He would charge his attacker down.

The scout staggered, and then he leapt to the left, but the black mare's hooves caught him, and Hruidgar, still bent low in the saddle, drew his short sword and swiped.

He hit nothing. It was too short for a cavalry blade, and not meant for striking a man while mounted.

Cursing, Hruidgar leapt from the saddle. He could not let this man escape, for then he could give warning to his comrades and a whole group of them would be after him.

He hit the ground running, but the scout had no intention of fleeing. Blood showed on his tunic, but whatever wound he had did not seem to slow him down much. He charged himself, and the two of them met in a crash of steel blades.

It was not a pretty fight. Neither were great swordsmen. Hruidgar wished he had a tenth of the skill with a blade that Brand had, but he had to settle for what he possessed.

What he possessed might be enough. Maybe. He hacked and blocked, and the other man did the same. There would be no fleeing now. To turn was to invite a sword blade through the back.

The other man was younger. Much younger. But he was wounded, and his breath came in ragged gasps. It evened out the age difference.

Suddenly the other man stumbled back. Hruidgar drove forward, his blade seeking the scout's life, but it was a ruse. The man had drawn a knife and he flung it hard.

Hruidgar dodged to the side. This time, he heard the knife pass close to his head and even felt the wind of it. He moved to attack again, but he had been thrown off balance and the other man leapt forward, his blade thrusting at Hruidgar's heart.

Hruidgar stumbled back in his haste, and while he escaped the killing stroke, he also lost his balance. He fell down, landing badly.

The sword came for him again, this time a wild slash at his neck. Somehow, Hruidgar fended it away, and the smash of steel on steel was loud in his ear. But the other man was standing over him, and Hruidgar kicked him in the groin with all the strength he possessed.

The enemy scout groaned and staggered back, bent over. Hruidgar rolled to his feet and struck. The man was little able to defend, but grunting and lurching backward he fended off the blows. Most of them, at any rate.

One slash hit his left shoulder, and there was the grating feel of metal against bone. Hruidgar had hoped for a killing stroke, but this was not it. Nor was it debilitating, for it was not his opponent's sword arm.

A moment later, the tip of Hruidgar's sword nicked the man's thigh. It drew a yelp of pain as well as blood, but again it was not a killing blow.

Hruidgar pressed forward. He had the advantage now, and he tried to take it. But the other man was facing death. And he knew it. He fought back with tenacity born of desperate fear.

Once more Hruidgar nicked him, this time a shallow slice across his stomach, and it seemed to enrage the other man. Either that, or the desperation of his situation drove him to one last attempt at victory. He crashed forward, screaming and slashing wildly.

Hruidgar was forced to retreat. This time he kept his footing, and blow after blow smashed against his sword until the hand that held the hilt grew numb. But he blocked all the attacks, and the other man grew weary. A great lethargy seized him. And Hruidgar realized his enemy must have lost a lot of blood. Death was creeping up on him, and that had lent the man desperation.

But it was nearly over now. The man swung slowly, and the power of his blows was much reduced. Yet still determination set his face in a grimace, and he advanced with a fierce expression that did not match what his body was able to deliver.

Suddenly, Hruidgar felt sick. He was going to kill this man, and he did not want to. Not like this. But he steeled himself. The man had probably been the one who killed Durnheld.

Before he knew what was happening, his own blade turned from defense to attack. It drove forward and up, slipping into flesh and seeking toward the heart.

The blade tip found it. Blood sprayed from the man's mouth, splattering over Hruidgar's face. He wanted to jump back, but instead he stepped closer, forcing the blade higher and twisting it.

His enemy fell, dead, and Hruidgar reefed his sword free, with difficulty, and then turned and vomited.

For some while he emptied his stomach, and in moments between he used a rag he carried to clear the blood off his face. But all the while he kept his sword drawn, and his gaze swept the countryside seeking other scouts.

At length, he recovered. Standing, he surveyed the countryside all around again, but there was no sign of any enemy. Not that he could see much anyway. Dusk had nearly given way to night.

He walked over to the man he had killed, and he knelt next to him. In the last of the light he studied his clothes and weaponry. All were different from anything in the Duthgar. They were different from anything he had seen before. Without doubt, he was of that race of men that the stories called the Kirsch.

But what amazed him most was the man's footwear. They were not boots, but something he had heard of in stories. Sandals.

He stood and shook his head. The clothes and weapons were well made, but sandals were foolish.

Perhaps they would serve in hotter climes, but when summer faded, which it nearly had done, frost and snow would set in. Sandals would lead to frostbite. But not only that, a sandaled foot was vulnerable in battle compared to a booted one.

Hruidgar gave a low whistle. His mount was some way off, having been scared by the fight. It was no war horse, nor ever would be. But its ears pricked and it studied him. Then it shook its head and the reins dangled down loosely.

He needed that horse. It was speed, which was the one thing he required above all else. He had much yet to do before he returned to the camp and gave Brand warning.

The horse looked at him, but it did not trot over. No matter. He would go to it. But slowly and carefully. He could not afford to spook it.

He took a few steps, and spoke quietly. Night was all around him now, dark and dangerous. The black mare was one with it, and though she was no warhorse, she stepped quietly when walking and had a turn of blistering pace when pressed to it. Both might be needed in the long hours to come.

He stepped closer again, talking softly and calmly. The blood that was on him would not help. He had cleaned it off as best as possible, but she could smell the stain of it on him, and she did not like it.

But she responded to his voice and took a few halting steps toward him.

He paused himself. "That's right, girl. Come over here. We have a long way to go, you and I, but I'll see you there safely if you do the same for me."

She shook her head again and stepped closer once more. He stayed where he was. She was a quiet animal and well-trained, but if he scared her now he could end up searching for her half the night.

He kept talking and she stepped over to him, stretching out her neck and sniffing at him.

Slowly and carefully he reached out and gripped the reins. When they were in his hand, he breathed a sigh of relief and patted her shoulder.

"Good girl," he said. "Remember our bargain. I'll look after you, and you look after me."

He mounted then, and looked around into the dark. There was little to see. Even the corpse of his enemy was just a darker shadow among many on the ground. Best not to think about that. It could have been him. And it might yet be if he was not careful.

What to do next? It was a pressing question. His goal must be to find the enemy encampment, for surely there must be one. Where the scouts were, the army could not be that far behind. His task had not changed. He must estimate their numbers and try to deduce their intent.

He nudged the mare forward, staying clear of the corpse. His thoughts were all about the enemy somewhere ahead, but a part of him knew there would be other scouts out in the dark. Perhaps there was no one around for ten miles. Or perhaps there were a dozen moving in on him now. It was impossible to tell.

He did what he had done before though. He moved quietly, or rather he allowed the horse to pick her own way and move at her own pace. It was slow, but it was near silent. And now and then he guided her to a different angle to avoid being predictable. But all the while he moved southward.

The enemy was in that direction. If they were more to the south-west, it did not mater. His scouts were roaming that territory, and they would discover the enemy if they were there. But here, it was just himself and those other few men he had sent this way. But of them, there had been no sign and he feared they were all dead.

104

The night grew cool. Autumn was drawing on, and though the days were still warm the night made promises of the winter yet to come.

He scented the air often for smoke, for surely the enemy encampment would have cooking fires. But he detected nothing. That did not mean much. The air was near still, and the scent of smoke would not travel far. And if anything, the breeze was coming from the north. Not that there was much of it.

Instead of smoke, he must listen carefully for the dull noise of an army ahead. He would hear them before he saw them. But the closer he drew, the greater his danger would be. Once he was in proximity to any encampment, it was not just scouts that he had to look out for but sentries. If he stumbled into one by accident, he would be dead before he could blink.

He could not slow the horse further, but he pulled her up often just to stare into the dark and listen. But he heard nothing save the hoot of owls and the scuffling of small animals in the leaf litter beneath trees. He did not fear the noise came from scouts. A scout would be silent until the attack came.

It grew even cooler, and he drew up the hood of his cloak. It was a risk, for the cloth dulled his hearing and reduced his sight. But all life was a risk, and he felt that his luck was in. He had, after all, survived the ambush by the enemy scout.

The oaks about him began to grow thickly now. It was nearly a forest here, and he did not think the enemy would establish a camp in such a place. The commander would prefer a spot in the open where a view was obtained of the surrounding countryside. Trusting to his luck again, he urged the mare forward at a faster walk. The night was wearing on, and better for him if he found the enemy at night. He could get closer that way, undetected. During the day it would be harder.

The oaks loomed over him, and the shadows were deep. It was the middle of the night, and drowsiness set in. He wanted to lie down and sleep beneath the cover of the trees, but duty pressed on him. Brand needed to know what was going on here, and swiftly.

The yearning for sleep passed. The oak wood around him thinned, and the glitter of stars lit the sky again. They were old friends to him, and he knew them well and the stories that were told of them in the Duthgar. Different stories were told in Esgallien, and other lands between. But some of those stars and the stories of them had been the same wherever he traveled.

He did not look at them tonight though. His eyes searched the shadows ahead, and his ears listened to his backtrail. But it was smell that told him what he wanted to know.

The air was perfectly still now, and the scent of old smoke was suddenly heavy upon it. The enemy camp was close, and though he had thought to hear it first, he had been wrong.

But if he could smell it, it must be close indeed. Not even the faintest breeze blew now, and there was nothing to bring the smoky air to him. Gently, he pulled the mare to a stop.

If he were afoot, he would have hunkered down here in the grass and waited. But he must trust to the night and the dark coat of the horse to hide him. Yet still, he did not know where the enemy was, only that they were close.

Dimly, he saw the land ahead of him slope downward. Where he waited now must be some sort of ridge, though he had not known it in the deeps of the trees. He knew it now though, and knew also that it was a likely spot for an enemy lookout.

Nothing moved. Nothing stirred. And he could not wait here until first light revealed him to the world. He nudged the horse forward again, and soon he came to the edge of a drop.

It was not steep. But spread out below was a vast area of flat lands, blanketed by the night. Except for many hundreds of fires. Here, at last, was the enemy he had sought.

But how big was the army? Certainly, there would be many more men than fires. But how many?

The only way to find out was to go there and see at close range. But he did not move. Fear gripped him. There could be scouts anywhere. There *would* be sentries. The stupidity of trying to go down there undetected overwhelmed him.

But that was the shadow of fear upon him. In truth, he had skill. He could do what was required. He *must* do what was required.

He nudged the mare forward. It was colder than before, but he flipped back his hood. He would need his every sense to survive this, and he could not afford to dim them.

Quickly, he checked his knives and made sure they were all in place. He had many of them, and he was a good thrower. But preparation was king. So he strung his bow for the first time. Almost, he notched an arrow, but that was going too far. If he needed to act quickly, it would be at close range and the knives would serve him better.

Lastly, he drew a leather pouch from his belt and dipped his fingers into it. It contained powdered charcoal, moistened by oil. This he smeared onto his face. It was the most likely aspect of him to be seen, for the horse was black and his clothing dark. It was the face of a person that glimmered palely in the shadows, revealing them.

For good measure, he smeared some on the back of his hands too. It never harmed to be too careful. Then he gave all his attention to the night around him as he moved down the slope and toward the enemy.

18. The Enemy

Far away the approaching dawn colored the horizon gray. But daylight was still a long way off. Even so. Hruidgar hastened as much as he dared. He had to get close to the army, and then back into the trees before first light. Otherwise, he would have a whole regiment sent to kill him. Or worse, take him prisoner for questioning.

Travel was easier once he reached the flatter land below the slope. But there were few trees here and not much that offered cover. He relied on the soft walk of the mare to make little noise, and his senses to detect the presence of anybody in the dark with him.

The glittering stars were not quite so bright. The horizon had become grayer. Even, he thought that he could see further through the dark than he could before. He wanted to urge the horse into a canter, for time was running out on him. But that would be foolish. He gritted his teeth and pressed on as he was.

Suddenly, he paused. Drawing the mare to a standstill, he waited in silence. Had he heard something? Had some sense warned him of hidden danger?

He felt vulnerable atop his mount. Being higher, there was greater chance of standing out against the lighter sky and being seen. He wanted to dismount. Yet if he did that, and he was attacked, he could not flee.

And flee he would have to try to do if detected. There would be no fighting here, if he could avoid it. To fight here was to risk alerting others, and in a matter of moments he could be fighting a hundred men.

So he waited where he was, and listened, while his gaze swept the mysterious night.

Then a noise came from off to his left. It was a man clearing his throat. It was not loud, and perhaps the man was not even conscious that he made the noise, but he did, and it had saved Hruidgar's life. On such chances turned his fate.

Hruidgar continued to wait. It was several minutes more before the man once again cleared his throat. The noise came from the same place as it had before, and there was no sign of anyone else. How far away were the sentries placed? Would there be one line of them or two?

He had no answers to any of his questions. The only thing to do was move forward again. But now, he dismounted. He could not risk being seen. Being heard was already likely enough.

But the horse moved quietly, and the grass here was short and soft. Somehow, he moved ten paces, then twenty and finally fifty without any sign of being detected.

He realized that a cold sweat had broken out over his face, and his hands were clammy. His face did not matter, but clammy hands were dangerous. The bow could slip in his grip when he needed speed and strength.

Wiping his hands dry, one at a time on his trousers, he mounted again. Moving forward, he saw the army begin to take shape before him. The fires had died down, but they gave off a cumulative light, and he could see the silhouettes of tents and the rough shapes of men that lay beside the dying fires.

The tents were few. The men by the fires many. He drew closer, his gaze taking in everything that he saw. There were banners held high by spears stuck into the ground, but they were too distant and the night too dark to see any detail. Of cavalry, he saw no sign. It was an army of infantry, which was a good thing for Brand, and something he would wish to know.

Then he set to counting. He was close enough now, as close as he dared go. He eased the mare to a stop, but he did not dismount. He needed his higher position to see better.

He divided the army into eighths, and counted one portion. Then he did the same again, using a different portion. His count was close to the same, both times. Then he multiplied by eight. Three thousand of the enemy were gathered here.

It was an army. By the standards of the Duthgar, a great army. But was it all of the Kirsch, or just some of them? He did not know, and had no way of finding out.

It was not likely to be all of them though. It was not a large enough force to take on Brand by itself, though stranger things had happened. Probably, the enemy had split into two. This was supposed to be a surprise flanking force. That meant that the real army was likely to the south, as expected, and that it was bigger than this.

The realization was not comforting. Once again, Brand would be outnumbered. Yet at least he would not be surprised. So long as word made it back to him.

That was his job now, and Hruidgar knew it. Nothing else mattered. He *had* to reach Brand. But he had made it safely this far, and going out should be easier than coming in had been.

But he had to hurry too. Movement in the camp had begun, and preparations for a meal started. The fires were being fed the remainder of the dry wood that had been collected last night. Soon enough, the enemy would be on the move again.

Worse, the eastern horizon was lit orange by the rising sun. Daylight was close to hand, and he would have to hurry to make it back to the relative safety of the woods before he could be seen.

He used his knees to signal the horse to turn, and then he nudged her forward. Safety lay ahead, but to get there he must pass through the sentry line again.

Following the same path that he entered, he left. It did not seem as though the sentries patrolled the perimeter of the army. They stayed in place where they had been stationed. This would help him, or at least so he hoped. He could not be sure he was taking precisely the same path.

He eased ahead, conscious of the lightening sky behind him. All was quiet. Shortly, he reached the place where he had heard the sentry clear his throat on the way in. But there was no sign of him now. He brought the horse to a stop and waited, surveying the dark, but he could not wait long.

Satisfied, as best he could be, that he had retraced his route exactly, he nudged the mare forward again. But even as she moved a figure loomed up out of the dark.

It was the back of a sentry, but the man must have heard something for he turned even as Hruidgar watched. A moment they each looked at the other, both shocked to see what they did.

The sentry fumbled for his sword. It was a mistake, for he should have yelled. Or better, dived away and shouted a warning.

Hruidgar lifted his bow, notched an arrow and drew and fired in one motion.

The sentry wore armor. He was no scout, sent into the wild to find and observe the army. He was a warrior, and well-protected. There had been only one killing shot, and that was to the neck.

The arrow flashed, a dark streak in the dawn shadows. It hissed through the air, and then struck with a thud. The sentry reeled back, blood gushing from his torn throat, and then he toppled and lay still.

Hruidgar swiftly notched another arrow and then waited, perfectly still, listening for other sentries. Had they heard anything?

His heart thudded in his chest. The horse stamped restlessly, but no call came from another sentry asking if all was well, nor any sign that someone walked across to investigate.

But still, Hruidgar waited. Fear gripped him, but after some while a greater fear took over. He had to get out of here, and swiftly. Dawn was at hand.

He slipped the arrow back into his quiver, and he dismounted. Walking the horse forward, he came to the man he had killed. He knew what he had to do. Should he be left there, his body would soon be found and an alert given. That an intruder had seen them would be known, and it was best for Brand that the enemy thought themselves undiscovered.

It would be best for him to. If they knew he was here, men would be sent after him.

Quickly, he bent down and pulled the arrow from the dead man's throat. He cleaned it, and returned it to his quiver. Then he lifted the man over his horse's withers ahead of the saddle.

There was blood on the grass, and this he washed away as best he could with some water. He tried to leave no sign that a man had been killed there. It was possible that the other sentries would think he had deserted during the night.

It was the best he could do. He mounted again, and nudged the horse forward. He did not notch an arrow again. If he were discovered, he would kick the horse into a gallop and escape that way. However, he did slip a knife into his hand in readiness.

But he passed through the sentry line without further trouble. Yet still the knife remained in his hand for several hundred feet. He looked ahead to see any sign of the enemy, and he looked behind for any pursuit. There was nothing, and his nerve gave out at last. He heeled the mare forward into a trot, hoping to reach higher ground and the shelter of the oak trees before daylight revealed him to all the world.

The dead man draped over the shoulders of the horse before him bounced to and fro. It made Hruidgar sick, not least because in dying the man had soiled himself. But it was necessary to hide his body. This was war, and it was kill or be killed.

And yet the Kirsch had begun it. They had no business here, and Hruidgar hoped with all his heart that Brand could defeat them. If anyone could, it would be him. Even so, he would be outnumbered, and he would face gods. Could a man prevail against such odds, no matter who he was?

Hruidgar looked back. It was light enough now to see the army, albeit dimly. Fear gripped him, and he kicked the mare into a gallop. A chance gaze could reveal him now.

He sped along. The horse labored slightly under the weight of two men, but the animal was all class. In moments, it was climbing steeper ground, and soon after it had cleared the crest of the slope and entered the shelter of the oaks.

Hruidgar drew the mare up and turned her around. From within the shadows of the trees, he looked back and observed the enemy.

There was no sign of anyone separating from it to hunt him down. Not on horseback nor on foot. It seemed strange to him that they had no cavalry at all, but it was an advantage to Brand and he liked it. Even more did he like that the army showed no signs of agitation. It seemed that the missing sentry was either unnoticed or caused no great concern.

The tracks of his horse were another matter. They would be visible for anyone with the skill to see. But those with the skill were probably out scouting and not nearby. At least he could hope so.

Finally, he turned the mare around once more and nudged her forward into a walk. Now that the surge of fear had left him, he felt exhausted. He had gone a long time without sleep, and he knew he would have to rest soon. But for that, he would have to find a well-hidden place deep in the woods. There also he could hide the body of the sentry.

He moved on, fighting sleep and trying to stay alert to the woods about him. The army was no danger anymore. Certainly, their scouts had found the edge of the woods and they would march near there and in open country. But that did not mean that scouts were not infesting this wood, ensuring no enemy lay concealed within it, nor that they would not stumble across his tracks.

The morning passed, and the warmth of the day grew. It was cold nights and warm days this time of the year. But soon it would just be cold. These foreigners and their sandals would struggle then. But if they were here at that time, they would have beaten Brand.

He managed to stay awake and travel until noon before weariness overtook him. But when he dismounted, deep in a stand of oaks, he hid the body in a hollow tree just as the enemy scouts had done themselves. So too he covered the opening with a large branch and hid his tracks as best he could.

Finally, he cast himself down and slept. If there were scouts around, they could kill him for all he cared just now.

But he slept undisturbed for several hours, and when he woke, dusk was settling over the land and he felt somewhat refreshed.

He did not bother to eat. He mounted the mare and set off. He still had a long way to go, but the dark offered concealment now, and he was far enough from the army that enemy scouts would be few and far between.

19. Five Tribes

Brand had led his army onward, and others had gathered to it. Now that it was known that several Callenor lords had joined him, others who had hesitated did likewise.

The army swelled, but his fears did not lessen. The task ahead was too much for him. He was a man, and not a god. Yet the Lady of the Land had charged him with the task, and this she would not have done if there were no hope. She had said as much herself.

So he went on, gathering warriors, building morale and establishing a sense of unity. None of it was easy, and there was no let up at night.

Dusk had fallen, and he had picked a place to encamp. He now had a tent, large enough to fit his entire group of commanding officers, but he did not use it. Instead, he sat outside on some logs before a blazing fire and listened to the reports of the scouts as they came in.

And for the first time, they brought word of the enemy army.

The third scout to bring news of it that evening sat before him now, close to the fire. Brand had given him a chunk of bread and goblet of mead as he made his report. The scouts were always grateful for that kindness. They came to him to report as soon as they entered the camp, and they did not tarry to eat or drink first.

"How large is the army?" Brand asked.

The scout sipped at his mead. "Seventeen thousand strong, in infantry. But there are five hundred chariots."

This was very close to the figures the previous two scouts had given. The numbers were a concern, but even more so the chariots. Brand had heard tales of them, but formulating an attack or defense against such a novelty was not easy.

"These chariots," he questioned, "how do the enemy use them?"

"Most are drawn by a single horse, but a few by two. Behind is the chariot itself, and for this there is a driver and a warrior."

This also Brand had heard before. "And what weapons does the warrior have?"

"He's armed with a sword, but also with a short bow. Possibly they could skirmish, but I think more likely they'll approach our lines, fire volleys of arrows and then wheel away again."

That too, Brand had heard before. He deemed it most likely himself, but it never paid to be sure of things that were not proven.

"And the driver?"

"He carries a shield, likely used to protect them both, and a sword also."

Brand offered the man another chunk of bread, which he took. "You've done well. And your tally of the enemy's numbers matches the other scouts so far. Rest well tonight, for no doubt you'll be needed again tomorrow."

The man nodded and walked off.

"They don't say much, those scouts," Shorty commented from where he sat nearby.

"No, but they never do. Scouts are quiet men, as a rule. But what he said was enough."

"Do the chariots trouble you?" Taingern asked.

Brand shrugged. "All things trouble me, until they don't. But the short bows of the charioteers won't shoot as far as the longbows of our archers. They'll think to swing past and soften us with volley after volley before sending in the infantry. But they'll get better than they give."

"I think so too," Shorty answered. "But they'll be a moving target while our men will be standing still."

Brand knew that was true, and he did not like it. "Agreed, but even so I think we'll at least match them. And we can hope they'll be surprised by the power and range of our bows."

Attar stretched out his legs where he sat on a log. "You Duthenor think too much. When they come at us, we'll shoot them down. It's that simple."

Brand grinned. "I like things simple, and you're probably right." He did not add that time would tell, but despite his simplistic approach, he knew that Attar did not underestimate the enemy. He just did not believe in worrying about things he could not change.

It was not much longer before another scout came in. Brand gave him the customary goblet of mead and a chunk of bread.

"What news," he asked.

"I've been to the north," the man answered. His voice was the deepest Brand had ever heard. "There's an army there."

This was something new. Brand studied the man as he sipped at his mead. He was one of the few Duthenor to wear a beard, and it was thick and black.

"How large," Brand asked.

"A thousand strong," the man answered without hesitation. Brand liked that. It spoke of confidence. And certainty that he had seen what he had seen and made the correct calculations.

"Who are they?"

"I don't know. Callenor, I expect. But they flew no banners."

"Cavalry?"

The man shook his head. "They're all foot soldiers. And they're close. Less than a day away."

It was interesting news. Brand had thought all the Callenor who were going to join them had done so already. They were nearing the end of their lands.

The scout had little else to report, and left soon after.

"Do you think they're Callenor?" Brand asked Attar.

"They'd better be. They're on Callenor lands. But in truth, I wish I was sure. I would have thought that all the Callenor who were going to join you had done so already."

Brand was uneasy about the whole situation. It was not a large enough force to threaten him, but he did not like mysteries. Not when it came to war and battle. In the game of swords, the unknown was a greater threat than blades.

But the mystery was solved not long after. Bruidiger returned from his mission to the Norvinor tribe. He came straight to Brand, and Brand shook his hand in the warrior's grip.

"I bring good news," the man said.

Brand poured him a goblet of mead and handed it to him. "Let me guess. You've led a thousand men to join me?"

"Ah, I see. Your scouts have spotted us. I'd thought to surprise you."

"Well, it's still a surprise. We knew a force was out there, just not who it was. But surprise or not, it's good news. Better than I'd hoped for, and quicker."

Bruidiger quaffed his mead in one go. "Things went better than I expected. Still, these are only men from the southern regions of our land. There'll be more to join us from the north later."

Brand refilled the man's goblet, and filled one for himself too.

"I'll drink to that."

Bruidiger quaffed the second goblet as fast as the first.

"There's something else too. With me I have a hundred men. Most are from the Waelenor tribe. But a few are from the Druimenor tribe."

Brand had heard the names of those tribes growing up, but he had never met anyone from them. He grinned, and quaffed his own mead.

"That's fitting. They may be few in number, but all five tribes will now be represented. I like it, and their swords will be welcome."

Brand called over a soldier then, and he sent word to the men who had made the last banner. He wanted a new one, and this time to represent the emblems of all five tribes.

"If men will die fighting in this army, however many or however few from each tribe, they should at least fight under a banner that means something to them," he said to Bruidiger when the soldier left on his errand.

Bruidiger did not answer, but he looked knowingly at Brand. He was another who thought a kingdom was being forged here, but he did not seem disturbed by the notion.

Taingern leaned forward and pointed. "Over there, Brand."

Brand looked. Walking toward him through the camp was Hruidgar, and he looked the weariest man Brand had ever seen.

"That man has been through it," Taingern said.

Whatever *it* was, Brand had no idea. But he agreed. Something had happened. But underneath all the weariness of the hunter, something else showed. Determination.

Hruidgar reached them, and once again Brand poured out some mead.

"You look like you need it," Brand said.

Hruidgar took the goblet. But he merely held it in his hand and did not drink.

"The enemy are close," he said.

Brand nodded grimly. "Yes, they are. But your men have already warned me of it."

Hruidgar seemed confused for a moment. Then he shrugged.

"What have my men told you?"

"Seventeen thousand in infantry," Brand answered.

Hruidgar considered that. "And they're coming in from the south-west, as expected?"

"Exactly so."

"Well," Hruidgar said softly. "I haven't been out that way. I went south instead."

Brand felt his stomach sink. This would not be good news.

"I saw an encampment there of three thousand soldiers. They had no cavalry."

Brand did not show any surprise, though he felt it. A commander must be seen to take all news in his stride.

"What about chariots?"

"Chariots? No. Nothing like that. Does the other army have them?"

"They do."

"Well, that's some luck then. Nasty things according to the tales I've heard."

Brand posed his next question carefully. "You're the first to report this second army."

Hruidgar dropped his head, and then for the first time sipped at his mead.

"I thought I would be. The enemy has good scouts. I found one of my men. Dead. Dead, and hidden. That was what warned me. So I went ahead, but carefully. I had a feeling I was the only one to see the army. Or at least the only one to make it back to tell you. But I got lucky."

Brand knew that was an understatement. The hunter had certainly been lucky, but luck was one of those things that the harder you worked and the better your skills, the more of it came your way.

He filled the hunter's cup with more mead, and gave him some bread.

"Rest, Hruidgar. You've earned it. But if word comes in of any other scout from the south, I'll let you know."

The hunter left, and Brand's mood soured. But such were the ups and downs of war. A little while ago he was happy that more were joining his army. Now that good news was overshadowed.

"Your thoughts, gentlemen?" Brand asked.

"They'll try to flank us," Shorty said. "When the main battle comes, they'll drive in from the side."

Taingern nodded agreement. "But they'll try to keep their presence hidden as long as possible. Even, if they can, right up until the moment of attack."

That was certainly true. Hruidgar had said their scouts were good, which was no easy feat in foreign terrain. These lands must be nothing like their homeland.

But even so, surely some of Hruidgar's men would have avoided them. The enemy had deployed not just skilled scouts, but many, many of them. And for the purpose of ensuring their flanking army was *not* observed. That indicated they intended to launch a surprise attack, just as Taingern thought.

But knowing what the enemy planned was one thing. Countering it was another altogether.

He knew what needed to be done though, even if he did not like it.

Brand looked at the men gathered around him. He trusted them all, but who had the skills to do best what would be required?

Only Shorty and Taingern. But which one of them, both great friends, must he send into terrible danger?

20. There Goes a Good Man

Brand spoke into the silence. "You know what needs to be done."

He did not direct the comment at anyone in particular, but both Shorty and Taingern nodded.

"I'll do it," Shorty answered.

"I'll go," Taingern said at the same time.

Sighern swung his gaze from one to the other. "*What* needs to be done?"

Brand turned to him. "The enemy is out there, preparing to flank and attack us when we engage their main force."

Sighern considered that. "So you'll send a force to oppose them? And either Shorty or Taingern will command it?"

"Exactly. But we're outnumbered. So against three thousand, I can only spare one thousand. But, despite their superior numbers, this might be enough. They hope to catch us by surprise. Thanks to Hruidgar, they've failed in this. But they probably don't know it. So, in our turn, we can hope to catch *them* by surprise. A smaller force can more easily achieve that. And we have Callenor warriors who know the country. That's an advantage to us."

"But it'll be dangerous?"

"Extremely. If the force is observed and surprise lost, they'll be in great jeopardy. But they won't be able to retreat. They *must* engage the enemy as the enemy is ready to engage us. Or our whole army will be at risk."

Sighern answered quietly. "I see. I'm no great warrior, but I offer my services. I'll go with either of them."

That took Brand by surprise, but he knew he should be used to it now with Sighern.

"You're a better warrior than you know, but I think I'll keep you here. You're my flag bearer, and I have plans for you."

He turned to his two oldest friends. "Which of you will it be?" he said simply. "I can't choose."

Shorty grinned at him. "Then you go, and we'll both stay here." He finished this with a wink, showing he wasn't serious.

Taingern laughed. "I'm not sure that going is any riskier than staying. But I'll flip you for it."

He withdrew a gold coin from his pocket, and turned it side to side. The image of Unferth was on one aspect, and two crossed swords on the other.

"Take your pick," Taingern said.

"Swords," Shorty answered.

"Then I'm heads," Taingern said, and he flipped the coin high with his thumb.

Brand watched as the coin turned and tumbled through the air, reaching a high point and then falling. How it fell would determine the fate of one of his friends, but in the end all life was chance such as this.

The coin landed with a thud. They all bent lower to look.

The gold visage of Unferth gleamed back at them.

"I never did like him much," Taingern muttered. "But maybe dead, he'll bring me more luck than he ever did alive."

Brand sighed. "Let's hope so. But you make your own luck Taingern. You always have."

Taingern retrieved the coin. He weighed it in his hand a moment, and then handed it to Shorty. "Keep it for me until I return."

Shorty took it. "I'll do that."

"We'd better discuss a few things," Brand said.

Taingern sat again. "It seems simple enough. Take a thousand men. Move swiftly, but undetected. Attack the enemy force just as they're about to attack you, and turn their attempted surprise on its head. This will not only nullify their flanking move, but also throw out the main force from the south who'll be relying on the chaos caused by the flanking to drive forward their own thrust."

Brand sat down as well. Taingern always did have a quick grasp of strategy, and he showed it here.

"It's the *undetected* part that concerns me."

"How so?" Taingern asked.

"The whole plan depends on it, but it's the hardest part to actually do."

"I don't get it," Sighern interrupted. "I'd have thought a thousand against three thousand was the hardest part?"

Taingern answered him. "Numbers count less in battle than you might think. Morale and preparedness are worth more, any day. If I catch them by surprise, their superior numbers won't mean much at all."

Brand agreed. "What he says is right, and it's a lesson worth remembering. But to move undetected will mean taking Hruidgar with you. He's our best."

"He's tired now, but he'll have a full night's sleep. He'll be right to go."

"He can take the majority of scouts with him too."

"The majority? What if you need them yourself?"

"You'll need them more. To catch the enemy by surprise, you'll have to kill any scout that might find you. Besides, I have a feeling the army coming from the south-west won't maneuver too much. They'll make themselves obvious and draw us in to battle quickly so that our attention is on them. That's what I'd do to draw focus away from scouting in other directions."

127

Taingern thought about that. "You're right. And I'll need the scouts, but with a bit of luck I'll be able to fully circle this flanking force. Their scouts will be ahead of them, between them and you. They'll not expect someone coming up behind them."

"Exactly, but that raises a point. Their scouts will already have observed us. But they don't need to see you going. Leave just before dawn, and head north first."

"Into Callenor lands?"

"I think that's best. If any scouts *should* mark your going, let them think you're abandoning the army. Let them think anything but the truth."

Taingern grinned. "A good idea. And perhaps better if they do see us go. Then they'll take word back to their leaders that there's discord in our camp."

"The greatest weapon in warfare is deception," Brand quoted.

They fell silent then. The plan was made, and it was up to Taingern and the men he chose to fulfill it. But all plans were fragile, and subject to the tides of chance.

"Good luck," Brand said.

Taingern stood, and Brand shook his hand in the warrior's grip.

"Best of luck to you also."

Taingern left then. He had much to organize, but he shook Shorty's hand also before he departed.

"Keep that gold coin safe. I'll want it back."

"I'll try not to gamble it away," Shorty said.

Then Taingern disappeared into the dark of the camp. As he left, Sighern watched him.

"There goes a good man."

"The very best," Brand agreed.

Brand issued orders then. First, he sent word to the scouts in the camp that they were to go with Taingern.

And then he sent a man to Hruidgar, if he was still awake, to tell him what had been decided.

21. The Golden God

Char-harash paced to and fro, and anxiety evidently gnawed at him. He muttered to himself also, but Horta did not catch the words.

This much was evident though. He was stronger than he had been, and the previous night's hunt had sustained him in some manner. But also, he did not like the sun, and he was careful even as he walked to avoid any patches of light that shone down through the gaps in the tree canopy above.

But why should a god be anxious? What did he know that might make him so?

Char-harash spun upon him. "How powerful is this Brand who leads the enemy?"

"In magic, O Great One?"

"Yes, in magic. But in all things."

"He is not like others I have known. He has strong magic, but it is not like the magic of the Kar-ahn-hetep. I don't understand it well. The power seems to come directly from the land without working through a god. He uses no rites or ceremonies. But he is powerful. Perhaps a match for me."

"Can he fight gods?"

Horta felt a stab of fear. How could he answer such a question? The gods were powerful, yet they had failed several times trying to kill the man. But he could not say that, nor should he lie. Char-harash was likely to detect it.

"He has the courage to fight gods. And he always seems to be lucky. But luck runs out for all men, eventually."

Char-harash gave a brisk nod. "Luck can run out for gods too." His leather-dry hands clamped over his belly, and Horta remembered the legend. It was said he was killed by a spear driven into his guts and up into his heart.

"What else is there to tell of Brand?" the god-king demanded.

"He's a skilled leader of men, both in a military sense and a political. He has courage and determination. His people … like him."

Char-harash grew agitated. "It seems as though you admire this man?"

Horta thought on that. "I do. What is the point of enemies if they don't test you?"

"That may be so. But gods do not have enemies. They crush them like a man squashes a beetle beneath his foot. And I would just as soon that Brand did not exist. He vexes me, and he defies my brothers and sisters yet."

Horta began to have an idea of why Char-harash was anxious. It seemed he had a way of communicating with the other gods, and that they had not defeated Brand yet. But the army of the Kar-ahn-hetep could not be far away. Battle would be joined soon, and his people would be supported by gods. How could they lose?

The god-king was not done speaking though. He raised his voice and lifted high his withered arms. But it seemed to Horta that he spoke to the universe rather than him.

"I shall prevail," he said, and his hands clenched into bony fists. "I shall be the Golden God, bright as the sun and my benevolence will make the earth prosper wherever my armies have conquered. But winter I shall call down upon my enemies. The grains of the earth will shrivel and rot. The rivers will stagnate. The frosted earth will bear no fruit. These things I will command, and the earth will obey, or she will perish in defiance."

131

A moment the god king stood, still as a statue, his gaze cast upward, and then he swung again to Horta.

"I feel the strength of star and planet run through me. I am invincible!"

Horta had long since given over his belief that the gods were invincible. But it would not do to say as much. Nor did he think this creature before him would be a Golden God. Rather, he would be a Dark God. But that thought he crushed lest it showed on his face.

He bowed. "You need no servant, Great Lord. Yet still I offer my talents, such as they are, for your use."

"All will be well," Char-harash answered. "My children come to me, and my brother and sister gods work to one purpose, as they rarely have before."

"Yet still," Horta found himself daring to say, "Brand is an opponent of strength and cunning. He seems to find a way to defy powers greater than himself. How it is so, I don't know, but it is something of which to be wary."

The god-king showed no emotion. Instead, for once he seemed to consider the words rationally.

"He is the champion of the land. That is why. And that is all. It need not concern us."

Horta had heard of such a thing before. It was said that in ancient days the Letharn had such champions. Then it occurred to him that the Letharn prevailed in those times against all the might of the Kar-ahn-hetep. Could it be so again? Could his people and his gods be defeated once more? All things were possible under the sun, but that was hard to believe. Brand really was just a man. He could not continue to defy gods.

Char-harash leaned in close, the dry sockets of his eyes boring into Horta.

"You said you are my servant?"

"Yes, O Great One."

"Will you do anything I require?"

"Of course. You are my god."

The dusty gaze of the god-king turned to Tanata.

"And you? Are you prepared to give whatever your god requires?"

"Yes," Tanata said simply. But he trembled as he spoke, and his bow did not cover it.

Horta saw the way that the god looked upon his Arnhaten, and he had a feeling Tanata's days on earth were growing short. There was a burning hunger in that long-dead gaze. The god would consume him in sacrifice. A poor fate for one who had served so well, but it was not his place to question. He was a servant, and it was his role to obey. But still, he was sick of such waste.

22. Let Them March to Us

Brand led the army forward, and it marched into uninhabited places now. No tribe claimed this area, though the road of the Letharn built long ages ago continued.

But even the road seemed little more than a path now, for it was narrow and rutted and grown over in places by bushes and trees. Yet still it took them south-west, whence the scouts reported the Kirsch were located and were hurrying on themselves, as expected.

That morning the thousand that Bruidiger had brought joined Brand, and Brand had met Arlnoth, chieftain of the Norvinor tribe. So also he had met representatives of the few among the new warriors who were of the Waelenor and Druimenor tribes. These were strange men to him, at times much like the Duthenor but also different. Yet they looked good fighting men, and after the initial reserve of their first meeting was gotten over, they seemed at ease and ready to fight for their lands with the others.

Brand had given Sighern yet another banner to carry, and this had the emblem of all five tribes upon it. The red dragon of the Duthenor, the raven claw of the Callenor, the radiant star of the Norvinor, the crossed swords of the Waelenor and lastly the eagle of the Druimenor. Sighern carried it proudly.

For the first time, Brand felt the army was coming together as one. All the tribes were represented, and with word of the enemy ahead the lords had stopped bickering. There was only one thought now. Fight together as one, and turn away the enemy.

They stopped for a noonday rest atop a hill with a long view. They could not see the enemy, but the scouts kept coming in reporting their movement. The Kirsch hastened toward them.

The Norvinor chieftain approached Brand. "Battle will be joined soon," he said.

Brand liked the man. He reminded him of Taingern, because he was red-haired and freckled. But his manner was always thoughtful too.

"Soon," Brand replied. "Soon indeed. But there's no need to hasten it. Let the enemy come to us if they will."

"You think they'll attack us on a hillside?"

It was a question Brand had given much thought to. "I think they will. They know the longer they wait the more chance for their flanking force to be discovered. I think they'll attack quickly and try to employ the advantage they believe they have."

The existence of the flanking force had not been kept secret. Better that the men knew and were prepared for it. All the more so if Taingern's counterstroke was defeated.

"They have the advantage of numbers," Arlnoth said. "Even so, they'd have to be confident of beating you to attack uphill."

"I agree," Brand said. "But they *are* confident. The scouts report they march straight toward us, and swiftly."

The Norvinor chieftain ran a hand through his red hair. "It sure looks like they'll attack. But they might change their mind when they see us. They might have the greater numbers, but the five tribes gathered together is no small force."

Brand turned his gaze to the south. At the base of the hill lay a large wood, and it was this more than anything that gave him confidence the enemy would engage. It was perfect cover for their flanking force, and he did not think they would let that chance slip by. At least, so long as

135

Taingern remained undiscovered. If he was able to do so, then the trap would be turned around on those who sought to snare him.

Shorty had been listening. "Of course, there's another tactic available."

"Go ahead, Shorty."

Brand knew that what would come next would question his own tactic. But that was good. That was Shorty's job.

"This is a good place to fight. The hill is to our advantage, and so too the creek to the north." He swept his hand out in that direction, and Brand knew what he meant. The enemy would be funneled toward them, uphill all the way.

"But numbers still matter. We're fifteen thousand strong, less now the one thousand that Taingern leads. The enemy is seventeen thousand strong, with five hundred chariots, the effect of which we don't properly know."

"That's correct," Brand agreed. "We're outnumbered, and we have no way to factor in exactly how the chariots will be used against us."

Shorty continued. "The standard rule in warfare is to avoid engaging a greater force. And here, we do have the option of avoiding battle. We know where the enemy is, and we can retreat from them."

It was an option Brand had considered. "We could, but that would expose our lands and people to the mercy of the enemy."

"It would. But it would also allow time for more forces to join you. Perhaps in a few days or a week, you could match the enemy force warrior to warrior."

"Perhaps," Brand said. "But there's no guarantee of that. But this much *is* certain. Winter is coming on. The enemy is far from home. To whom will they turn for supplies of food?"

Arlnoth folded his arms across his chest. "They'll turn to Norvinor lands. Or Callenor lands. Or whoever is nearest at the time. They'll ravish farms and towns, seeking food and supplies and killing indiscriminately."

The Norvinor chieftain seemed certain of this, and he had made up his mind that it was best to make a stand here.

"We don't know any of that for certain," Shorty countered. "The enemy will have a supply route, linking them to their homeland. No army would march without one."

"Agreed," Brand said. "But supplies for an army are never enough. Even our army, so close to home and support, is struggling. Supplies are *always* fewer than needed, and likely the enemy would do as Arlnoth suggests. And if not for supplies, perhaps just to spread terror before them."

Shorty shrugged. "What you say is true. All of it. For myself, I'd pick this place for the fight as well."

Arlnoth scratched his head. "Then why did you argue against it?"

Shorty winked at the chieftain, but it was Brand who answered.

"That's his job. The job of all in my leadership team. I don't want followers. That's a sure way to find defeat. I need people willing to speak their mind and offer alternatives. Even if they agree with me, I want them to suggest other ways of doing things. That way all options get considered."

Arlnoth raised an eyebrow. "That's an interesting approach. You Duthenor sure like to make things complicated."

Brand grinned. "That's something I may have picked up in Cardoroth. Things are not so simple there. But they're not simple here either, I guess. The only thing we know for sure is that people will die. That's our only guarantee. As for tactics and strategies, the only true test is the battle."

23. I Will Not Kneel

The army encamped, and threw up ditch ramparts to fortify its position. It was wasted work if the enemy did not attack, but if they did, it would go some way to balancing out the numerical superiority of the Kirsch.

The work went well, and the army ate well overnight and rested, enjoying a break from Brand's fast-paced marches.

By dawn, more scouts returned. The enemy came on, unswerving. It was a beautiful day, but marred by the threat of war and the pall of anxiety that hung in the air. No army was ever free of that. Not when a hostile enemy was nearby.

The night had been cold again, but the day warmed swiftly. The sky was cloudless, and it seemed the height of summer weather was here. But winter was approaching, and with it snow. The Kirsch, even if they won this war, would be ravaged by it.

Brand turned the possibility over in his mind. If his army lost, the five tribes must fend for themselves. There would be few warriors left. The Kirsch would move to confiscate food and shelter. But what would the people do?

It would be hard, but they would flee into the hills and remote places. They would take what food and livestock they could with them. The rest would be destroyed to deny it to the enemy.

It was a grim thought, but if the Kirsch won here, they would face a harder battle later. But it was not something to dwell on. It was Brand's task to ensure the enemy did *not* win here. That was what he must concentrate on.

And he had made a good start. He had a favorable position, now further fortified beyond what nature had provided. The creek protected them well on one side. The woods on the other were a deadly trap, but for him or the enemy was yet to be decided. The prospect of it would draw the enemy to attack when perhaps they would not otherwise. But there were three great unknowns that troubled Brand.

The first was the gods arrayed against him. He had seldom known defeat before, but they were a force above him. The second was the chariots of the enemy. Against them, he could take steps, but not with certainty. The third was Taingern. He trusted no one else except Shorty to do the job that was needed, but it was a hard task. If Taingern failed, Brand knew he would face a superior enemy on two fronts.

The enemy was not visible, but soon the dust cloud of their passage showed. It hazed the air, and then it grew thicker as time passed. This, perhaps, was due in part to the chariots. The horses that drew them and the wheels of the chariot itself disturbed the ground more than marching men.

No doubt, it was a reason that the flanking force did not have them. It would have been much harder to try to approach in secret.

Eventually, the army itself came into view. That it was large, Brand already knew. But it really did seem to hasten.

Attar noticed the same thing. "They're keen to join battle," he said.

"Or trying to give the *impression* of being keen to join battle," Sighern offered.

Brand turned that thought over in his mind. It was entirely possible. The enemy may yet hasten toward them only to halt a distance away and fortify a camp of their own. Or they may skirt his force altogether and force him to leave his advantageous ground. All things were possible, and he was glad that Sighern had considered such a thing.

But his instinct was that the enemy was supremely confident. This, perhaps, was the influence of their gods. They would come, and they would attack, and they would expect to win. Why should they not?

The enemy drew closer. Flashes of metal shot through the air. The movement of a great mass of men was visible. And the chariots also. These were deployed as cavalry often were, broken into two units and forming the outer wings of the force.

Brand, once again, set his mind to how they would be used. Their disposition was a clue. There were only two hundred and fifty to each side. Was that enough to use separately?

He did not think so. Despite being placed to each flank of the army, they would both be used in the same manner. Just like cavalry, they would charge, draw close to their opponent's ranks, and send forth volleys of arrows. Then they would be on their way again. Moments later, the second group of them would do the same thing. In this way they would take turns at harassing his army and intimidating it. When their general thought they had been softened enough, he would charge with the infantry and try to destroy all opposition.

That would be their plan. But how to counter it?

The enemy might suppose the speed and movement of the chariots made them harder to hit with return fire. This was so, and that the chariot driver also carried a shield would work into this. But they would not be expecting the stronger longbows of the five tribes.

Brand could use this by ensuring his archers shot the moment the enemy came into range, and before they expected attack. This would go some way to unbalancing their own attack. Also, the Duthenor and other tribes were skilled with shields. They would raise them high as a protective roof when the enemy finally drew close enough to shoot. They would not be as harassed or intimidated as the enemy general hoped.

The enemy would drive home their full offensive then, and that would be the real test. Against this, Brand arranged the Duthenor at the center of his defense. They had fought much lately, and they were hard men who would not be broken easily. The Callenor and other tribes he placed on the wings, but some also in the center. That way all the tribes fought together.

Under a warm noon sun, the enemy drew to a halt half a mile away.

"Will they attack or send an envoy first?" Furthgil asked, stroking his silver beard.

"It would be normal practice to send an envoy," Brand answered. "But who can say? These warriors are not like us."

They did not have long to wait. Five chariots came forward, and the lead one held a banner. It was a black scorpion, tail raised, against a white background.

The chariots drew up a hundred paces from the army, and two men dismounted and stood before them. The one on the left wore simple clothes. He was not dressed as the other Kirsch, and appeared taller and of another race. The one on the right was a commander of some sort. His bearing said as much, and his armor, though strange to Brand's eyes, was expensive and trimmed with gold as was the scabbard of his sword.

The tall man on the left spoke, casting his voice loudly and speaking in somber tones.

"The Kar-ahn-hetep have come," the man declared. "These lands are now theirs. Who speaks for you, and leads you, conquered thralls?"

It was not a gracious speech. And the accent was strange, dominated by whatever language the Kirsch spoke, but there was a hint of other accents in it too, some not unfamiliar to Brand's ear. He also noted how he had been placed in the position of one answering to the names of conquered and thrall.

"I lead this army," he replied. "This army of free men, unconquered. And if you think words alone can make us thralls, you are mistaken. The price for that will not be foolish boasts voiced into the air, but paid in spilled blood. If you have the heart to try."

There was silence for a moment, and then the tall man spoke again.

"Proud words, but in vain. You cannot stand against us. Surrender, and offer yourselves up to the mercy of the god-king to be. That you may know him, his hallowed name is Char-harash, Lord of the Ten Armies, Ruler of the Thousand Stars, Light of Kar-fallon and Emperor of the Kar-ahn-hetep! Kneel now to his emissary, Wena, and he will intercede on your behalf."

Brand did what no one expected. He laughed, and the shock of it showed on the faces of the foreigners.

"Char-harash? A god to be? You set a lot of store in a dead man. Yes, I've met him, or his spirit at any rate. He's a thing of dried rags and half-rotting flesh in a tomb. You can kneel to the shell of a man if you want, and pretend he's a god, but I'm a free man and I will not. Nor will my people. They are free also."

Brand drew himself up. And he cast his voice back over to the enemy, carried on a thread of magic that made it loud and deep.

143

"You are not welcome. Go back whence you came, and take your bickering gods with you. We will not endure them here. Should you not heed this warning, blood will flow in rivers and the might of your army will be crushed. Heed my words, for they are no threat but prophecy."

Brand fell silent, and he let the threads of magic that had supported his voice drift away. His concentration was on the second man on the right. So far, he had been silent. But unless Brand missed his mark, he was the commander of the enemy host.

The emotions on the other man's face were hard to read because of the distance, but even so Brand thought he saw shock or outrage at his reply gradually turn to anger.

The herald would have spoken again, but the second man stopped him with a swift gesture. He stood forth a few steps, and he laughed.

Brand knew it was false. This was a man of show, and not very good at it. But that did not mean his military leadership was poor.

"You will see," the man replied haltingly, and with a heavy accent. "You will see, and you will regret."

That was all he said. But his voice was confident, and Brand knew the man believed what he said. But even as he turned and remounted the chariot, his head swiveled to the south and the woods that lay there. All was silent there now, and nothing moved. But Brand sensed his enemy's expectation.

The chariot turned and sped back to the army, and the four chariots with it followed in its wake. When the commander reached its ranks, trumpets blew and a tumult sounded.

Shorty grunted. "That Wena doesn't say much. But what he has his herald say, I don't like. He'll please me better when I thrust a sword in his guts."

"Which one – Wena or the herald?" Brand asked.

"Both!"

Brand did not really listen to the reply. He knew Shorty only spoke to relieve the tension of the men. His thoughts were on the wood, and especially on Taingern. So much depended on him.

24. First Blood is Spilled

Char-harash sat atop a boulder in their forest camp, and Horta watched him carefully. For some while the god-king had been excited, muttering to himself and shaking his head. Horta began to wonder if he was sane.

But that was a stupid thing to ponder. He was to be obeyed, no matter what. And if he was not sane? What dead person come back to life in a far later age than he had lived would be? Horta considered it all. Why should he care one way or the other? So long as he remained careful, he would enjoy the spoils of victory at the side of a god.

The god-king turned to him, and fixed him with those dry sockets that served as eyes.

"The battle prepares," he said. "Listen, and learn, for I shall show you now of the old magic."

Char-harash turned away then, and fixed his gaze to the south-west, though there was nothing to see there but trees. But in moments, he began to chant.

His voice was different. It was softer, almost as though he mumbled. It was not a summoning of a god or a beseeching of divine aid. That would not be fitting anyway for one that would be a god himself. Horta did not know what it was, for it was not like any rite that he had ever heard or read of.

Yet there was magic in the words. He felt the power of it build and grow. He tried to memorize what he heard, but Char-harash continued to mumble and he could not catch all that was said.

That too was a difference. Most of the rites that Horta knew rose to a crescendo as the power was unleashed. Yet not so here. It was almost as though the god-king drifted away to sleep. And, after a little while, his mumbling grew so soft as to be inaudible. Then it ceased altogether.

Nothing happened. Char-harash continued to sit there, but now his head was bowed. Perhaps he was meditating.

But suddenly his head snapped up and his back stiffened. He spoke again, his voice strong now, though with a faraway cast to it.

"The Children attack!" he proclaimed. "The Sons of the Thousand Stars bring war as once they did of old. These lands that once were nearly ours will assuredly fall this time."

Horta exchanged a glance with Tanata. Could the god somehow sense what was happening elsewhere? But they dared not speak, for Char-harash was not done.

"I feel the rush of blood in my veins, and what it is to be a man in battle. The battle cry that rises in their throats, rises in mine. The thrumming of their hearts sets mine afire, and the hatred in their minds as they charge is as kindling to my spirit."

Horta understood now. Somehow, Char-harash saw events exactly as they were transpiring elsewhere.

This was the final throw of the dice, and the culmination of everything that Horta had so long worked for. His people were coming, and his god had wakened and walked the earth once more. Yet he felt empty inside, for he knew what was to come.

"Horses and chariots fly over the earth," Char-harash declared. "The hooves are thunder and the wheels rumble. Sharp are the points of the arrows to be shot, and they glitter with the fire of the sun. Ah! The glory of battle is here and the earth will be wetted with the blood of my enemies."

This now was the hour of Brand's downfall, and Horta should be pleased. Yet he was not. Had he been in Brand's place, would he not have done the same things?

"First blood is spilled!" Char-harash proclaimed, and there was excitement in his voice. "Now also my brothers and sister come, and they lend their wills to mine."

The god-king sat even more upright, as though his back were a rod that had just been thrust upward, and his bony hands clawed at the stone of the boulder. It seemed that he struggled, either living out the battle being contested or striving for the strength to maintain the magic that he wrought.

"Now I see afar," Char-harash said, and there was hatred in his voice, "he who leads the enemy. Brand! How I hate him! But his day has come. He shall be as dust beneath the sandaled feet of my children."

Suddenly Char-harash sprang upward to stand upon the boulder. He was a towering figure, and menace and power radiated from him. For once, he appeared to be the god that he claimed.

"The enemy is struck. Ah! The glory of it! Blood flows, and yet it is but a taste of all that is to come. Kingdom after kingdom. Nation after nation. Land after land. All will fall to me!"

The god-king stood there, radiant in his power, but in the blink of an eye he seemed lesser again. He fell to one knee and held up his hands imploringly. "No! My strength lessens, and the vision fades."

With head bowed once again, but his dark eye sockets still visible, he turned his dead gaze on Tanata.

"Come to me, my child."

Horta looked at his acolyte. Tanata trembled all over. There was fear in his eyes, and had he been able he would have run. Yet some power held him, and he stepped, slow pace after another, toward his god.

With certainty, Horta knew what would come next. Life gave power. Sacrifice nourished the god, and this was the first of many.

25. Worthy of That Axe

Brand watched, and it seemed that the very earth trembled at the charge of the enemy host. No trial of strength and resolve was this. It was a full attack, and no reserves were left behind. This was army against army, steel against steel and man against man. The stronger would prevail. The weaker would perish.

Afar, he heard the trumpets of the enemy. But they were drowned by the rushing of the chariots. They would strike first, unleashing their arrows, but such was the confidence of Wena in victory that the army followed. One attack only the chariots would launch, and Brand, despite the cold that had seeped into his bones, rejoiced at the mistake. The enemy did not know the danger of his archers and their longbows, and Wena would not learn of it until it was too late to halt the charge.

But still, though the longbows would take a great toll, it would not stop such a charge as this.

The chariots roared closer. They came from each wing of the enemy, but the left group had begun sooner and would reach first. When they had passed, then the right group would take their place.

The faces of the chariot drivers were visible now, and so too the warriors standing beside them. Hard men all, and skilled. Brand marveled at the horsemanship and the balance of the men to ride such a vehicle and yet still be able to use their weapons.

Closer they came, and Brand studied the small recurve bows they held. He glanced at his own archers. They had moved, according to plan, to the front rank of his army.

There they stood. Proud men, and hard also. No less than the enemy, nor suffering from lesser skill. Arrows they had notched already, and in moments death would flash through the gap between opposing forces.

Brand waited. Fear thickened the air all around him. It was always thus in battle. A horn blew in his front ranks, and others took up the note. The archers did not draw their bows. Rather, they kept their right hand at rest and pressed the weight of their body through the left. This bent the limbs of the great bows that only strong men, trained since their youth, could shoot.

And then they shot. Long arrows hissed through the air. One hundred yards. Two hundred yards. Further still, and the enemy, unready, rode into a storm of death.

Hurriedly the drivers raised their shields, protecting them and their passenger. But caught by surprise, many shields were not well placed. Arrows slew men. Armored horses died also. Chariots and beasts fell in tangled wrecks, and screams ripped the air.

The enemy came on. Arrows flew again. The charioteers were better prepared now. Not so many died, yet still screams roiled up into the heavens. A litter of dead and dying lay behind the wheeled charge, and this would do little for the morale of the infantry that followed.

Three times the archers shot, sending death to the enemy. Then they raced back between the ranks of the army. Now, the charioteers were in range with their own bows, and these they fired as the chariots wheeled in a part circle.

Shorter arrows, less deadly, now flew. Less deadly, but deadly enough. Despite the raised shields men still died. But fewer than among the enemy.

Brand watched, calm as ever. He would die today, or he would live. Victory would be his, or loss. His army would conquer, or be vanquished. All he could do, as with all his men, was try.

He glanced to the other group of chariots. These, coming in a little later, had not been so devastated by his archers. But he saw fear on the faces of drivers and warriors. Their charge was not so swift. They too drew close and unleashed their attack. More of Brand's men fell. But not many.

The chariots raced away. Brand's archers, having sheltered behind the last rank of infantry, sprang forward again. They would have little time, but the enemy infantry came on, and they would receive at least two flights of arrows.

Brand willed speed to his archers. And they did not disappoint him. They moved with alacrity and precision, coming to the front once more and firing a hail of arrows at the charging host.

Men went down, only to be trampled by those who came after. It mattered not if they were dead or alive. But many were dead, for the arrows found targets between lifted shields. No shield wall could be properly held during a charge, and it was yet another mistake of this Wena. The enemy should have approached at a steady march, thus protecting themselves better.

Three volleys Brand's archers managed before the enemy was nearly upon them, and they withdrew once more through the ranks of their comrades.

Those ranks closed swiftly, shield to shield and man to man. Then, with a mighty roar, the two forces came together in a deafening clash. Men died on both sides. Blood spurted and guts spilled to the earth. The dying screamed and the living yelled their defiance.

The center of the army where the Duthenor mostly stood began to buckle back, ceding the advantage of the ditch rampart. This was where the enemy attacked the most fiercely, and Brand surmised that Wena had done as he had also done, placing the most experienced warriors in the center.

Sighern held the banner of the five tribes higher. He looked at Brand, and Brand read the question in his eyes. He wanted to know if it was time for Brand and his leadership group to bolster the men by joining them.

"Not yet," Brand told him above the din of battle. "The men will hold this charge."

He hoped it was true. The line buckled further. But if he joined in now there would be nothing to give later. And also, he must keep an eye on *all* his enemies.

The three gods of the Kirsch that he had met before were there now, behind their army and urging it forward. What plan had they concocted? What sorcery would be sent against him? He must keep himself free as long as possible to face that threat.

The buckling line steadied and then, slowly, pushed back. The Kirsch screamed their battle cries, fighting inch by inch, for they sensed how close they had been to overrunning their opponent.

But they had not. And the quick victory they had sought, even expected, did not happen. Almost, Brand could feel Wena's chagrin.

The three gods were not still. They moved about behind the ranks of the Kirsch, urging them ahead and filling them with purpose. If not, with fear, for the men redoubled their efforts.

Again, the line began to buckle. This time it was the left wing. Brand's gaze flickered to the woods. Should the second army of the Kirsch attack on that flank now, all was lost. But there was no sign of movement there.

Shorty too was looking in that direction.

"We hold!" Sighern cried. "We hold and push them away again!"

Brand turned back to the battle. The left wing was creeping forward once more, and a great shout went up from those ranks. The joy of battle was upon them, for they had faced death, defied it, and now turned it onto their enemies instead.

Brand knew that feeling. But such was always the ebb and flow of battle.

So it proved. On and on the battle raged, and no quarter was asked nor given. Again and again Brand's lines buckled, but always some hero stood forth and rallied the morale of the men, bringing them with him to straighten it. Sometimes, though much less often, the defenders pushed forward beyond the earth rampart, opening a gap among the enemy.

Whether this was a tactic of the enemy to draw them into a trap or not, Brand did not know. But he never gave an order to capitalize on it and try to break the foe. If it were a trap, this was what the enemy wanted. If not, and he thought not, his army was not big enough to rout the enemy in that fashion. If he were to win, it must be by holding and wearing the opponent out. Only when they retreated might they be vulnerable to attack.

And always, the gods were there. Vague glimpses of them from behind the enemy. Moving. Cajoling. Perhaps threatening. They used no magic that Brand sensed. Their presence alone was a kind of magic that gave purpose to the enemy and offered support.

But that could not last. The gods would make their own move against him at some point, and even as he watched his men straighten the line once more and stand resolute, Brand knew that moment had at last come.

The gods acted. A spell was loosed. It drove the Kirsch to a frenzy of attack, and hatred was in their eyes and an absence of fear in their hearts.

Brand did not wait for the lines to buckle against this new threat.

"Now!" he cried to his leaders. And the lords of the five tribes and the chieftain of the Norvinor sprang forward with him. Before them all Sighern lifted high their banner.

"Now!" Brand cried again. "To battle and war and the defeat of the enemy!"

And some in the ranks of his men heard his great voice above the tumult, and they called out to others to tell them, and his joining of the fray and that of the lords lent strength to weary arms and courage to desperate hearts.

Brand moved forward, and a way was made for him and those with him to enter the ranks and come up to the battle line itself. Above them Sighern held the banner of the five tribes, but not for long.

He drove the spear point into the ground and stepped forward into the front rank also. Brand saw him on his left, and he was glad that he was there. The young man had courage, and he wielded the light Raven Axe with skill, using it to stab with its spike like a sword.

Brand was glad also that Shorty was on his right, and together they fought with sword and shield, firming the line against the frenzy that came against them.

The Kirsch were maddened. The influence of their gods drove them, and some even threw down their shields to swing their swords two-handed.

This was an error, and the power of the gods turned against them. For these warriors were swiftly cut down, though they died slowly, clawing forward over the ground even as they perished to try to deliver one last strike against their foe.

Others of the enemy were not so careless of their lives. They fought with skill and determination, and the power of the gods did not make them reckless, yet still it gave them heart and purpose, driving them forward implacably.

The line began to buckle once more, despite Brand's presence. He fought with cool skill, stabbing and blocking, blocking and stabbing. Shorty did likewise beside him, and the dead enemy filled the lower ground before them.

Had Brand not ordered an earth rampart dug that gave his men an advantage, already they would have been routed. Even so, it would not be long now and Brand knew it. He thought desperately of what he might do, but even as he did so Sighern yelled a battle cry beside him.

To the lad's left fought Furthgil, that gray-bearded lord of the Callenor who once had been Brand's enemy and was now his ally. The man was older, yet he still fought well. But a blade had torn into his thigh from a near-dead warrior on the ground before him.

Half into the ditch Furthgil had fallen, and about him the enemy gathered for the kill. But Sighern dropped his shield and jumped down among them, swinging the Raven Axe of the Callenor wildly but to deadly effect.

The foe shrank back from him, and a Duthenor warrior heaved Furthgil up to safety. With a roar Sighern swept in among the enemy, causing them to scatter, for his axe severed arms and cut heads off the enemy in single strokes. Then the young man leaped back up to the line again and picked up his shield once more.

Brand looked on with pride. The boy had become a man. And a great one, for he had risked his life to save another.

Furthgil rose to his feet. A moment he held Sighern's gaze. "You're worthy of that axe, boy. Thank you."

Sighern nodded. There was no time to answer for the enemy came forward again. But a great cheer rose up round about for the courageous deed. And for all that the enemy pressed home their attack once more, thereafter they were wary of the young warrior with the deadly axe and tried to avoid him. Their drive had diminished.

The battle wore on. Here and there, Brand had an opportunity to glance southward to the woods. What was happening there? Had he miscalculated and the second Kirsch army would attack from another direction? And what of Taingern?

The gods tried a new tactic now. Or, more accurately, the Trickster did.

Brand noticed movement among the back ranks of the enemy, as though they made way for something or someone. He had an idea what this would be, and he was proven correct.

Gormengil pushed his way forward. He was clad in black, and a black-bladed sword was in his hand. He stalked through the Kirsch like a hunting animal, all litheness and deadly force ready to pounce. Yet his face and eyes were visible below his helm. And for all the liveliness and grace of his every move, they remained flat and dead.

Those eyes fixed Brand, and he felt a chill run through him. Magic was at work, but they gleamed with single-minded determination also. He had come to kill one person, and one alone.

Like a wolf after prey he came straight toward Brand, and it seemed that the battle raging all around them slipped away into oblivion. There was only the two of them in the world now, and nothing else mattered. The fight that they had not quite finished back in the Duthgar would be ended here.

But if Gormengil was already dead, how could he be killed and defeated? It was a haunting thought, and one that Brand suppressed. Doubt fed weakness, and here in this fight he must be at his strongest. Nothing else would serve.

But the thought remained. Even his strongest might not be enough. As a man, Brand knew he had Gormengil's measure, but as some magic-enhanced warrior it was another matter.

Gormengil drew up before him, shouldering aside Kirsch warriors, and his voice came cold and clear, a match for his dead eyes.

"Hail, Brand. Chieftain of the Duthenor and Callenor both. Are you ready to die?"

"Were you?" Brand answered swiftly. "For I killed you once before and I shall again."

Gormengil gazed at him with those dead eyes, and Brand knew this was a man beyond taunting or unbalancing. Perhaps even beyond fear and pain.

"Words," the one-time leader of the Callenor said, "are a poor weapon for warriors. Come! Let us put blade to blade and dance the one true dance."

Brand nodded. His shield he cast down, for Gormengil had none, and around Brand the men in the line made space. The black-clad warrior leaped nimbly up to the top of the earthwork rampart and there faced him.

Brand made no move to stop it. Single combat was an honored tradition among all the tribes, even in the midst of battle. Had he tried to stop it, men would have thought him scared and weak. This, he could not afford.

But single combat was a two-edged sword. Should Gormengil lose, the five tribes would rally all the harder behind Brand and try to emulate his example.

About the two combatants the battle went on, yet neither side fought with full attention. Every man tried to catch a glimpse, here and there, of the fight between the champion of the gods and the leader of the defenders.

Gormengil held forth his black sword, and Brand touched it with his Halathrin blade. A cold note rang out, and the duel commenced as if no battle existed but theirs.

Brand struck first. His sword swept low, aiming for his opponent's thigh where he had wounded him before. He had thought to remind him of that blow and perhaps cast over his enemy the shadow of doubt and a memory of pain.

But Gormengil seemed beyond such things. He stepped casually out of the way, a smile upon his lips for he understood what Brand had tried. But his eyes remained dead and void of all emotion.

Then the black sword flickered. It swept through the air and cut and stabbed. Gormengil seemed to make no effort, but the blade flashed with speed and power.

Brand retreated. He blocked and deflected, getting the feel of how his enemy moved. But he blocked and deflected clumsily, or so it seemed to him, for the other man was *fast*. Too fast for mortal skill. But this thought Brand put from him. He had faced deadly opponents before. Some that were better than him, and they were dead now. Skill was important, but courage was too, and a belief in victory. Not because it was deserved, but because others depended on it. That drove him on, and kept fear from his mind. He would not lose, because others needed him to win.

Gormengil dropped low and swept his blade out. Brand stepped back from a cut that would have crippled him, but the black-clad warrior was not done.

From his low position, Gormengil sprung upward into the air like a striking serpent, the tip of his blade flashing before him.

Brand stumbled back, surprised. It was a move that required incredible strength in the legs to perform. But to perform it so quickly was beyond human ability.

The blade nicked Brand's throat as he reeled away, and the fear of death was on him. How could he beat such an opponent?

But he must.

Anger coursed through him now, and he regained his footing and turned from defense into attack. His bright sword swept out, flashed and cut in glittering arcs and lines. Cold flame, pale as winter moonlight gleamed along its edges.

Gormengil merely gazed at him with those dead eyes, and he danced away and out of harm's way with ease. But Brand did not relent. He pressed forward, and his blade sliced the left arm of his opponent and his right leg also. Not deep, but enough to draw blood.

There was no change in the black eyes of his enemy. Neither fear nor pain showed. And soon Brand knew something else, also. The wounds did not bleed.

Was Gormengil dead? Did his heart pump hot blood? Or was he caught on the very cusp of death and held there, even unwillingly? The Kirsch seemed to have some fascination with death, and perhaps their gods shared it.

Brand feigned, ever so slowly, tiredness. Everything in battle and war was based on deception, and he feigned it well, for like lies the best trap was the closest to the truth, and his arms and legs were weary.

At the last, he stumbled for just a moment, the tip of his sword drooping lower than it should have. It was a snare. Well set and cunningly deployed. A thousand warriors would have fallen for it and rushed in to try to land a killing blow.

But not Gormengil. He stepped back instead, that smile on his lips again that was cold as the gaze of a hunting animal. But his eyes were not cold. For the first time they showed some faint glimmer of emotion. And it was contempt.

"Is that the best you can do? I had thought you a better fighter than that."

"Then come kill me, if you can."

160

"I can and I will. You know it. I see it in your eyes."

"And I see nothing in yours save what the goddess puts there. You are her puppet. Pulled on her strings. I had thought you a man, but you're a toy for her instead."

The black eyes hardened. Brand had guessed right, for there was chagrin there, and ever so faintly he felt the presence of the Trickster. But there was some other glimmer in those eyes as well. For just a moment he saw hope, and that was no emotion the goddess would be feeling now. Some part of the mind of the man that had once been Gormengil remained.

What that meant, if anything, Brand had little time to consider. His enemy swung a mighty blow at his head, and though he jumped back, still the edge of the blade glanced off his helm and a line of sparks flew, leaving a glittering trail.

Once more Gormengil attacked, and once more Brand defended, fighting for his very life and the hopes of five nations and lands unnumbered beyond them.

Steel rang against steel, and the thrum of the strikes traveled up Brand's arm and into his body. This was now no duel of finesse and skill, but a fight of hammer blows.

And Gormengil seemed not to tire. But Brand did. He tried to spare his body, but threatened as he was he must use all his strength and speed just to stay alive a little longer.

This was not a fight that could continue much longer. Brand knew he was outmatched, and sought now to use his magic to discover why. He could not, or would not, use it as a weapon against a man who did not threaten him with sorcery. Nor did he think that would work. The goddess would have given him protection against such a chance. Yet that did not mean that the means by which Gormengil was kept alive and given strength could not be sought out and considered.

161

Even as Brand retreated and the blade in his hand snaked out in defense, so too his magic slipped into the air and probed around his enemy.

The black blade was of steel, and no magic was in it. So also the armor Gormengil wore. Yet around him was cast a net of power, hugging him like water dripping from a man climbing out of a river.

And like a river, that power had a source. Fast as light Brand sent his magic probing along that current, seeking its origin to see if he could sever it.

Brand found it. He sensed at that place the joined minds of the three gods, and one other. This was Char-harash, the spirit that had hunted him in his dreams. He knew it, and recognized it, and anger flared even brighter. He was the root cause of the problems that had beset Brand ever since he returned to the Duthgar.

But with anger came frustration. The will of these four kept Gormengil alive, if life it could be called. Their magic animated his corpse, and kept his mind within it, trapped. He was like an insect frozen in ice, and the magic required for this was great.

Brand sensed the combined power of his four enemies, and it was greater by far than his own. The gods brooded behind the army, pressing them on and lending their strength to the Trickster whose will drove Gormengil. Yet also, from a great distance, the spirit of Char-harash strived the hardest. Somewhere in the Duthgar he stood upon a boulder in a forest and joined his will to that of the others.

The strength of Char-harash seemed to Brand to be greater, and upon him was focused a power of magic beyond Brand's experience. It was not of the earth as lòhrengai and elùgai were, but born of the cyclic powers of the universe itself.

Together, the gods were by far too much for him. And the instrument of their will, Gormengil, was thus beyond his skill and strength.

But he fought on, somehow avoiding the relentless death strokes Gormengil hammered at him. And he remembered the words of the witch. *Your enemy may yet be your friend. When despair grips you, hold tight to that thought.*

But none of these enemies were his friend, and all along the line the five tribes were pressed harder than they ever had been before.

26. Like A Torch

"Come to me, my child," the god-king repeated. And Tanata went to him, one slow step at a time, fighting each movement with all his will, but failing.

Horta watched. Tanata was but a puny thing compared to Char-harash. The one was a god, or a god that could be. The other only a man, and young at that. Nor deeply trained in the sacred mysteries. Not that training would have made much difference. But still he struggled, and valiantly. The instinct to live was strong, and the will of Tanata great.

Annoyance flickered across the leathery visage of Char-harash's face. He did not like it that his chosen sacrifice resisted. He did not like it at all.

From somewhere within the foul burial shroud the god-king wore, he withdrew a dagger. Hilt and blade were of gold, but dried blood darkened its luster. Last night Char-harash had caught prey to sustain himself, and now it was the turn of Tanata to lend his power to the gods.

Horta did not move. The sacrifice might as easily be his own. He did nothing to draw attention to himself, for that would be folly of the greatest kind.

But it seemed pitiful to him that one who would be a god looked as such. Dead. Dried to a husk. Smelling of corruption overlaid with the oils, resins, wood tar and sacred herbs of preservation. The hand that held the knife was a bony claw, and upon the boulder next to him was the war hammer with which he had broken from the tomb. Dead, but alive. Weak, but powerful. Hungry for power, but insatiable.

Of the two, Tanata was the nobler figure. The lesser fought the mighty, without hope of victory. But he did not give up, and Horta admired that.

His heart swelled. Tanata would be worthy to learn the sacred mysteries. But that chance was denied him. All chances were denied him. The god would consume his life to grow stronger, to see the battle that might decide his fate.

Tanata was close to the god-king now, and somehow he wrenched his head, so very slowly, to face Horta. He could not speak. He could do nothing but walk stiffly toward his own sacrifice, but his gaze silently implored help, and a single tear glistened on his cheek.

The god gestured impatiently with his knife, and Horta looked away. Some things did not need to be seen.

The forest was empty around him. No beast nor bird stirred. All was silent, and his heart was empty.

Had he served the gods for this? Death and destruction? Had he served them so that good men could die? Did he grovel at their feet, hoping to gather the scraps of their power? He did, and the voice of his heart that had long been silenced spoke.

He was a man. And he would live or die as such. Better to die thus than to live and know shame all the days of his life.

He swung around. His acolyte stood before the god-king, his head tilted up to expose his own throat. Charharash bent toward him, the gold knife in his hand held high.

Time ceased to move. Horta watched, transfixed. Not by the sight before him; he had seen men die before. But by the thought in his heart. It was blasphemy. It was death, for a man did not defy gods. It was an overturning of all that he had ever believed and striven for. If he acted on it.

165

Time moved again. The gold knife began to descend in an arc of cold death. The hollow eyes of Char-harash fixed on Tanata like a hawk on a mouse, and the dry tongue in his withered mouth licked his leathery lips.

Horta's hand was already in one of his pouches, and he had drawn a fistful of powder. Shouldering Tanata away and uttering a word of power, he flung what was in his hand straight at Char-harash.

Dust filled the air. It enveloped the god-king, but did not cover the surprise on his face.

Horta dived away. Char-harash made to leap from the boulder after him, but a thunderous boom rang out, and light flashed as though lightening tore at the earth.

And then Char-harash screamed. It was a horrible sound, as though all the agony the world had ever known was given voice all at once.

Horta lay in a heap on the ground. A wave of heat rolled over him and away, and he looked up through watery eyes.

Char-harash was like a torch. The white shroud of his burial was gone, but his body had caught alight and burned. All of it, from the stubby toes to his leathery face. The oils and resins and tar used to preserve his body in ancient days was flammable.

The god-king screamed, and fell to his knees on the blackened boulder. Greasy smoke coiled from his eye sockets, and sparks flew from his mouth.

Horta rolled away. But Char-harash screamed and leapt from the boulder, a streak of flame and roiling smoke billowing behind him. The earth shook as he landed, and he came for Horta.

Staggering, the god-king moved toward him. Horta got to his knees, but Char-harash towered above like a bonfire. And in his hand he still held the gold knife, heated red-hot as an ember.

The knife rose to kill him. This was the price of disobedience. He would be sacrificed himself. Yet still it would not save the god-king. Nothing could now. Those flames could not be put out, and already the corpse was falling apart.

The knife fell. But Tanata had come up beside them, and he held the war-hammer of Char-harash. With a clumsy movement he smashed at the god-king's arm and fended the blow away.

Char-harash turned on him and screamed, his open mouth gushing flame. But the hammer struck again, this time an overhead blow. It took Char-harash on the shoulder and sent him spinning. But the head of the hammer tore through his body also. An arm fell away. The head twisted at an unnatural angle. The torso was a ruin like a split tree trunk, and newly exposed embalmed tissue was fresh fuel for flames.

Char-harash tottered. He screamed again, though there was no sound now except the roar of flame. And he fell into a writhing heap.

There, on the forest floor, the god burned. And he did not cease burning, for the substances used in embalming did not flare and go out. Rather they would burn and smolder for hours.

Warily, Horta stood. Together the two men looked down on the remains of the god they had killed. If indeed Char-harash was yet dead. The body still moved. Whether that was the residue of life within him, or the heat of combustion, Horta did not know.

But there was magic to account for also. Chemicals had preserved the body, but magic had bound the spirit of Char-harash to it. That magic had endured through long ages, and Horta thought it would endure fire also. Until the body was consumed by the flames and become ashes scattered on the wind.

"Not a good way to die," Tanata said quietly.

"Neither was a spear through the body," Horta answered without pity. "But he suffered that. And he will suffer this."

27. The Hunter Becomes the Hunted

Taingern took his thousand men north into Callenor lands before the sun rose. With him were many scouts, and chief among them Hruidgar.

Much depended on the hunter. But more on Taingern himself, and he knew it. If he failed in his mission, Brand would likely die. And his army with him.

That was intolerable. The world needed Brand, and therefore it would not happen. He knew it for a vain thought, but thought was the root of action, and he would prove it.

He did not go far into Callenor lands. His task was to come around behind the flanking force and surprise them. That could be achieved in two ways. He could head north, traverse a great loop and come around again, all the while traveling at forced marches. Then, spent, engage the three thousand soldiers of the enemy's flanking army.

Or, he could wait where he was, resting and preparing, then when sufficient time had elapsed, and Brand's army and the flanking force had moved on, cut at a direct angle behind them. This meant covering far less ground and keeping his soldiers fresher. But it was also riskier. If he mistimed his march, the scouts of the flanking force would observe him.

But he chose this option. Decisively. He would take that risk, because he must face three thousand enemy with one thousand. For that, his men would need to be fresh.

Additionally, he knew his men liked the thought of resting while the enemy marched. It gave them a sense of superiority. It deepened the idea that they would outthink the enemy, and thereby outfight them.

Victory, just like thought, occurred in the mind first. Actions followed later.

Taingern knew others thought him cautious. The men were surprised at this plan, even if they liked it. But he knew himself better than all others. Only Brand and Shorty understood him. He was neither cautious nor adventurous. He merely did what was required. No more and no less. Usually, that gave him the appearance of caution.

But he could risk everything at need. And seldom had he, or those he cared for, had a greater need.

Hruidgar, perhaps, was beginning to understand him. But he knew better than most what was required here, and how it could be done.

The scouts were pivotal to everything. They must advance ahead of his force, identify where the enemy lay without being seen. Or, if seen, kill the observers. Without fail. All it took was one man to return to the flanking army with news of his presence, and surprise would be lost and with it the chance of success.

He waited until noon. The scouts were out long before that though. Giving a hand signal to the men, for nothing would be announced by horn in their current situation, he led the men back the way they had come this morning.

It did not take long to reach their old camp of last night. It was an empty place now, the army gone ahead with Brand toward the enemy and the destiny that awaited them.

Taingern turned that word over in his head. Destiny. If ever a man had one, it was Brand. But he denied it. A person made their own future, he always said. Perhaps that was so. But personal skill and courage only took you so far. The rest was design, or luck. But if there was no such thing as destiny, how then did prophecy work? And he had seen foretelling after foretelling come true about Brand.

His thoughts were disturbed as Hruidgar came and reported to him at the old camp, as arranged.

The hunter was not one for formalities. There were no bows or greetings. Taingern did not care. He had been on the receiving end of them for years, and knew them for empty gestures. The informality of Duthenor warriors, even to their leaders, was refreshing.

"So far, so good," Hruidgar said. "My men report seeing scouts following Brand."

"And the flanking force?"

"They're too far away yet. But they'll know their main force approaches. They'll want to stay as close as possible to Brand now. They'll go as close as they dare."

That was certainly true. Taingern did not think the main enemy host would delay. The battle was coming soon. It would be tomorrow.

"And have any of our scouts been seen?"

"Three, that I know of. But the enemy scouts who did so are dead." He gestured backward with his thumb. "The land out there is alive with my men. For the most part, the Kirsch scouts are staying between their flanking force and Brand. They're not concerned by the possibility of anything behind them."

Taingern nodded. "Let's hope we can keep it that way. Until it doesn't matter anymore."

Hruidgar grinned. "We just might pull it off. Then we'll see how they deal with a surprise attack themselves."

Taingern was not so keen. Once Hruidgar's work was done, his own would begin. And though surprise was a great advantage, he still had to lead his group against an enemy three times its size.

"It's safe for you to move out and cross the enemy's backtrail now," Hruidgar said. "But don't hasten. If there's any real catching up to do, it's better to do so with a night march."

"Of course," Taingern agreed. He knew the men would not like it, but they knew as well that the night would hide them. And they knew too that everything depended on surprise.

"Are you going back out now?"

Hruidgar looked grim. "I've got a personal score to settle with these Kirsch scouts. I'm going back out, and if I find any stragglers, they'd better watch out."

He said no more then, but just turned and walked away. Taingern liked it. The man had no sense of etiquette at all, but so long as he did his job, that did not matter. In fact, it reminded him of Shorty.

Taingern led his men on. They marched at an easy pace, in no hurry. But he made sure word was passed around that there would be a night march.

It was late in the afternoon, very late, when they finally crossed the trail of the flanking army. The signs of their passage were clear, and it confirmed that they were heading after Brand. Not that this had ever been in much doubt, but the possibility existed that their purpose was something else.

Night fell slowly, but Taingern did not halt the march. He followed the trail of the enemy, and he increased the speed of travel, bringing him closer to those he pursued. Ahead, his scouts were now concentrated. They ensured, or tried to ensure, that no enemy scout saw them. But as word continued to come in, it appeared that although the enemy was not watching closely behind them, further scouts had been observed and eliminated. Taingern just hoped that none had seen his approach unobserved.

The night grew chill, but the men did not feel it. He hoped that lasted, for there would be no campfires when they finally rested. Nor would there be any meals. There would be cold rations only. He made sure the men understood why this was so. Secrecy would preserve their lives. It was worth some minor discomfort, and the word back was that they agreed. This, and the secrecy of a night march, fed into the feeling that they were outthinking and outmaneuvering the enemy.

After some while, the dark grew ominous. Taingern ordered that the men walk quietly, and only spoke in whispers. It was an excessive precaution, but he felt it wise. The chances of the world were many, and all it took was one unseen enemy scout to hear a noise in the distance and come to investigate for the fate of realms to change.

It was a strange countryside, shifting between flats and small hills, alternating between woods and open ground. But the enemy had been careful to move as much as possible through the trees and had stuck to lower ground to avoid being seen.

Taingern followed in their trail, and he felt like a fox hunting a scent through the night. So it went, save for the regular rest breaks. But he was in no hurry. Word came back to him from the scouts that the flanking force was close ahead. But from Hruidgar, there was no word, and this was a worry.

Toward midnight Taingern called a halt. The battle would follow tomorrow, both his and Brand's, and the men needed sleep. They encamped in a creek valley, overgrown by trees. And the enemy was only a mile away, themselves in a wood, but one that bordered the ancient road whence Brand would be traveling.

It was a restless sleep, what sleep the men could even get. The camp was nervous, for everyone knew that battle and death, for them or the enemy, would play out tomorrow. But though they were fewer, and though they had marched part of the night, yet still their presence was a secret. If they could preserve that, then victory was possible when daylight came.

Daylight came swiftly. The scouts brought word that the enemy remained where it was. This indicated that they had found the place where they would launch their flanking attack on Brand. Soon after, word came that Brand was himself encamped on the road. Nor was he moving.

The three armies were coming together now, and Taingern felt the shadow of war and battle upon him. But it was good news too. Had they been forced to march again, during daylight and this close to the flanking force, the chances of being observed would have greatly increased. Now, they could rest and gather their strength. And they could do it close to the enemy in a good place of concealment. All that concerned Taingern was that Hruidgar still had not returned. If he had been taken prisoner, all their plans might be at risk.

They ate a cold meal for breakfast, but still a good one. No one went hungry, for that was a bad way to face a day that would bring a clash of arms. But they laid low, keeping quiet as possible. No one was allowed to leave camp except for scouts, and these now had been reduced to the bare minimum.

Only the best scouts now kept an eye on the enemy. The fewer there were out and about the less chance of them being observed. But that did not mean the remainder of the scouts were inactive.

These guarded the camp. And just as well. Two enemy scouts had been located and killed as they approached. Taingern could have wished otherwise, but it was what it was. They may not have seen his army and taken word back to their commander, but by their absence, and those who had been killed before them, suspicion would be raised. Taingern just hoped that the battle commenced before the enemy commander had time to consider the issue and act on it.

So it seemed to prove. For, at last, Hruidgar returned. He had been wounded, though not badly, and obviously at least one more enemy scout was dead. More fuel for suspicion, because the enemy must sooner or later realize their scouts were being killed and wonder why, but the news he brought was otherwise good.

"It's time, Taingern."

"The enemy is on the move?"

"Not yet. But soon. And they won't be going far. Everyone is converging on this spot, and the battle is about to be fought."

"How soon?"

Hruidgar glanced skyward. "It's noon now. At best, you have an hour to make your move."

Taingern considered that. It was enough time to cover the distance between the two armies. If only they could do it unobserved.

"How sure are you the flanking force is ready to attack?"

Hruidgar grinned, but the look on his face was a very grim amusement.

"They look as nervous as a rabbit caught in the open by a fox, and hoping he isn't hungry."

It was good enough for Taingern. If Hruidgar said the enemy were close to moving, it was high time he did as well. He trusted the hunter, but the enemy, even if nervous, were not rabbits.

He gave a hand signal, and the men, awaiting this, stood and fell in behind him. Taingern looked at them as they did so. They, too, seemed nervous. And no wonder.

175

Odds of three to one were very bad indeed. But they trusted to his leadership, and so far he had not let them down.

He vowed that it would remain so, and led them forward. As best he could, he tried to keep them out of sight, but the trees thinned in places, and any enemy could see his force, if they happened to be there. But Hruidgar, walking beside him, seemed unconcerned. Taingern matched his look, and slowly and surely they covered the distance. Then, faint and far away, came dim noises of battle.

Taingern quickened his pace, and he led his men on. Today would be a day of victory. Or of death. He was not sure which, but if needs be, he would die as close as he could get to Brand.

28. Advance!

Brand staggered, and the black blade of Gormengil whispered past his throat. But then Gormengil staggered too.

Through his magic, Brand still sensed how his opponent was supported by the gods, and by faraway Char-harash. The god-that-would-be stood upon a boulder, and he hungered for blood. His strength had weakened, and he drew a man toward him. And Horta was there also. But the magician had done the unthinkable, and attacked him. The pain of fire roared through Brand.

He withdrew his magic. But he had seen enough. Char-harash was mortally wounded, though it would take a long time for the magic that bound him to scatter, and all the while he would suffer unendurable pain.

The witch, once again, had been right. *Your enemy may yet be your friend.* Brand steadied himself, but Gormengil was still under the shadow of Char-harash's pain, and the dismay of the other gods had momentarily left him uncontrolled.

Gormengil swayed where he stood, and for once his eyes were not so dead.

"Free me," Gormengil pleaded softly, but Brand heard it above the din of battle and his Halathrin-wrought blade leaped out, severing the head of his enemy from its body.

Gormengil collapsed before him, but there was no blood. A great roar rose among the five tribes, and Brand thought it was for his winning of the duel. But only for a moment. He soon saw that battle had at last broken out in the woods to the south, and the flanking force had been attacked and driven into the open. There they were trying to make a stand, and yet some had already begun to flee to join Wena's force.

Taingern had fulfilled his task. But he still needed to win that battle. And Brand still needed to win his own.

It was not just the gods that felt dismay. The Kirsch must also feel it, for their secret attack had been foiled and their plan was unraveling before their eyes. On such chances and such moods the fate of battle rested. This, if ever there was one, was the time for Brand to grasp victory from defeat.

"Advance!" he cried. "Advance!"

Horns blew, sending his order all along the lines of his army, and they began to step forward. They would leave the advantage of the earthwork rampart behind, but that was a defensive position. Victory required attacking.

And attack they did. They rolled forward as a vast unit, pushing, fighting, killing. The enemy, surprised by the failure of their secret weapon, resisted less than they should have.

The balance had shifted. Both sides felt it, and Brand's army moved forward, down the ramp and beyond, harassing the Kirsch without mercy. Too late the enemy commanders saw the danger. Too late they tried to steady their ranks.

But the balance could shift again. If the enemy commanders regained their discipline, they could halt the slide. And surprise would not last forever. It was a momentary ally. Also, the enemy still outnumbered Brand.

Already there were signs that the advance was slowing. No soldier liked being beaten back by an inferior force. The battle still hung in the balance.

Brand knew what he must do then. It was a final throw of the dice, and a surrendering of trust to the words of the witch. She had not betrayed him so far, and he hoped it would stay that way. *Self-sacrifice is victory*, she had said. And he gambled on her prophecy.

Steeling himself and drawing on his well of courage, he spoke. And he enhanced his words with magic so that they carried across all the field of battle, back even to where the three gods of the enemy stood.

"Hear me!" he proclaimed, and his voice boomed like thunder. "I am Brand, and I challenge the three gods who lurk behind their army while soldiers, braver than they, die. I am Brand, and I would contend with you. All three at once, if you have the courage!"

A silence fell, vast and strange for its suddenness was unnatural in the midst of battle. But the battle had ceased. This was something beyond the reckoning of ordinary men, and shocked, they watched and waited in silence and fear.

Brand knew he must go on as he had begun. There was no choice. This was the moment to take advantage of the enemy's dismay. Char-harash had fallen, and if ever gods felt vulnerable, it would be now.

"Do you hear me, you three? Come forth and do battle, or be known as craven. Come forth and die, as your betters have done already."

The silence now was profound. Brand stood proud and tall, and there was certainty in his voice. It did not matter whether he felt it or not. Leadership was an act, and he could play his role. Let the gods wonder if he was mad or confident.

But the men near him trembled in fear. They backed away, leaving an open space around him. They wanted no part in what would happen if gods took offence.

Yet even so, three men came to stand beside him. Shorty first, and he glanced at Brand, his gaze unreadable. Sighern second, and though his face was pale he lifted high the Raven Axe and shook it defiantly. Third was Bruidiger, his sword wet with blood and a smile upon his face as though all the world were a joke.

An eternity seemed to pass. Brand did not move, and neither did the gods. They were wary of him, for their power had been lessened and the fate of Char-harash troubled them.

And then the gods were gone. Smoke, fire and mist swirled where they had been, and then drifted away on the air. He had called their bluff, for surely had they accepted his challenge, they would have killed him. But it seemed that gods were unused to exposing themselves to the chances of life and death. They did not have the heart for it, as ordinary people must, and their courage failed them.

Out of the silence a pitiful noise grew. It was the moaning of the enemy soldiers. Their gods had deserted them.

Coldly, for stricken as they were the enemy remained a superior force, Brand did as he must.

"Advance!" he cried, and there was no need for horns to carry the signal, for his voice, still buoyed by magic, carried across all the field of battle.

And the army of five tribes advanced, slaying the enemy before them and routing them.

Many of the Kirsch tried to flee. Some tried to gather together and retreat in order. Some fell in behind Wena, their commander, and these fought hardest. Or most desperately. In battle, it came to the same thing, and it was toward them that Brand came, his sword dripping blood and a cold fury in his heart.

No matter the doings and plots of gods, it was this man, Wena, who had led the enemy and sought to overrun and conquer lands not his own. It was Wena who had threatened to bring ruin to the five tribes and had asked for nations to kneel to him as their overlord.

Shorty and Sighern were with him, as ever. And suddenly Taingern was there also, blood smearing his face from a shallow cut to his head, his helm dinted, but a grim smile on his face.

There was no time for greetings, but a look passed between them. Then they were up and against the picked bodyguard of the enemy commander. These were tall men, dark-haired and broad of shoulder. Axes were their weapon of choice, and they bore no shields.

But swords and shields would have served them better. Brand's men beat them back, blocking deadly attacks and thrusting with their swords. These men, though brave, fell.

Then suddenly Brand was face to face with Wena. Hatred flashed in the other man's eyes, and Brand met it with his own implacable gaze.

Wena drew a sword, and he made to thrust with it, but then his other hand gestured and he uttered a word of power.

Brand felt the force of it. Magic was at play, and the taint of dark sorcery filled the air. His own powers stirred in response, but he saw nothing untoward. Yet still he felt something, and he leaped back.

Where he had just stood the earth crumbled in on itself and a fissure opened in the ground. Flames darted within it, and noxious gases rose.

Wena began to incant some further spell, but Brand was done watching. It was time to act, and to end this last battle. If Wena fell, all resistance would fall with him.

Brand discarded his shield, and leaped the fissure, his Halathrin-wrought blade glittering. Red tongues of flame twisted up to meet him, but he passed over them, and his sword flashed down and clove Wena's helm.

The enemy commander lurched backward, his split helm falling away and revealing his shattered skull. The white of bone showed through a mess of gore and brains, and then he collapsed.

The fight of the enemy collapsed with him, and the Kirsch fled the field.

"We have won!" Sighern cried, but he looked around at the ruins of the battle and the wreck of war, and the triumph on his face died.

29. Free of Ambition

The Kirsch fled, and the five tribes harried them until the sun set red in the west and a cold wind blew from the mountains of the north.

When dark fell, the fire went out of the hearts of the warriors, and Brand ordered a camp to be established and fires built. Tonight, they would eat and drink and revel in the life they yet lived. But also, they would remember who had died.

And there were many. Fields would lie fallow next spring that should be turned by the plough. Many were the warriors who would never tread the land of their farms again, nor milk cattle, grow crops nor harvest the golden ears of wheat as the seasons turned. Sons, husbands, fathers – the dead were many and the grief was great.

Simple warriors had fallen, but also lords. The names were given to Brand as news passed among men, and of those he knew he mourned the lesser and the greater alike.

Arlnoth, the red-haired chieftain of the Norvinor had fallen to a spear driven through his body. Yet in dying he slew his killer and two others of the enemy. Brodruin and Garvengil, both lords of the Duthgar had perished. The first killed early in the battle by a sword thrust to the groin and the second by an axe even as the battle was nearing its end.

The Callenor payed a price in blood also. Attar and Hathulf had both fallen, one to arrow shot and the other to a spear in his leg. It had not been considered a dangerous injury, but on moving back through the ranks to be bandaged, he had collapsed and died.

Brand knew he would learn more names of the dead as time passed, but for now he must care for the wounded. These had been gathered together and helped as much as possible. Brand went among them, but he saw that here and there men still died. Yet most, if they could, shrugged away their pain as he talked to them pretending that nothing troubled them though their skin was pale and blood seeped through bandages.

The long night passed in a strange blend of joy and grief. Few slept even a little, and Brand none at all. Yet the next day he felt strong. His task was accomplished, but there was still work to do and decisions to be made.

He ordered timber to be cut to burn the dead and stop the spread of disease. This was done, and long rows of biers were fired just before noon.

The fallen warriors of the five tribes were kept separate from the Kirsch, but the reek of smoke merged and drifted skyward together. The dreams of dead men went with it.

When this was done, the army rested again. Not yet were they ready to travel, and wagons and litters were being made ready to carry the wounded that could not walk.

But Brand and the lords of the various tribes met. Shorty, Taingern and Sighern were with them, and Sighern still bore the banner of five tribes proudly. He and the banner went wherever Brand did.

From the Waelenor and Druimenor warriors, few as they were, there were no lords. But the two most senior men were invited. Brand wished that all the five tribes be represented in any decisions made.

Small matters they discussed first, but needful. The care of the injured was uppermost in their minds, and the transporting of them to the nearest villages where they could sleep beneath a protective roof and feel the warmth of fires while healers were gathered to tend them.

But when this was organized, Furthgil, that gray-bearded lord of the Callenor spoke.

"Brand. You are chieftain of the Duthenor and Callenor by right. Yet you could be king, and I would have it so. And the people need you. If you announce this thing, it will give them heart and take their minds off the tragedy just past and turn it toward a brighter future."

Brand did not answer straightaway. And before he could, Thurlnoth, the most senior Norvinor lord there, for he was the son of Arlnoth with his same red hair, bowed. But Brand noticed that Furthgil had looked to him before the other man moved, and he knew this had been discussed before in private.

"I would swear fealty to you also, Brand. And call you king. I would serve under your kingship as a chieftain."

At length, Brand spoke. "To the lordship of the Duthenor and Callenor, I have a claim. But it is not so with the Norvinor. Why would you serve beneath a king?"

Thurlnoth answered without delay, and Brand knew again that it was a matter he had considered previously.

"Because the Norvinor are a small tribe, and as recent events have shown, the chances of the world are many. The Kirsch are defeated, but may they not come again? We have enemies in the north also. It is a world full of foes and uncertainty. A king, and being part of a larger realm, would offer us better protection against such things."

Brand thought on that. Then he turned to the men of the Waelenor and Druimenor tribes.

"What do you think of this? How would your chieftains react?"

It was a difficult question. If the Norvinor were a smaller tribe than the Duthenor and Callenor, then the remaining two were far smaller. They would fret at the thought of a kingdom forming on their borders, one that might annex them if they were not willing to join freely.

"We've discussed this with the others," one of the men said. "For our part," and he gestured to his companion, "we're just warriors. We can make no agreement nor say with certainty how our chieftains will react."

"But you can guess," Brand suggested.

The second man nodded. "It seems to us that our lords will see the advantages that Thurlnoth described. But at the same time, they would wish to retain their chieftainships over their own land, and rule there according to their own ancient traditions."

It was as good an answer as Brand would get without the chieftains themselves there. And he was sure these men would speak favorably. They had seen what the combined force of the tribes could do.

Brand took a deep breath. All his life it seemed had been driving him to this point, but having reached it, having kingship within his grasp, he did not want it. He was a lòhren, and the land needed him. And though the Lady of the Land had foretold that one day he would be a king, he knew now it would not be of the five tribes. His fate lay elsewhere.

He sighed. "All that each of you say is true. Truer even than you know. Our enemies are many. In the mountains north of us dwell evils untold. South, far, far to the south, a great darkness stirs. It grows and prospers. This I feel in my bones. The lòhren Aranloth has gone thither, and in time we will hear of great events. Hopefully, we will hear that the champion he will raise to stand against it is victorious."

He held back a moment on the last thing that he must say, assessing their mood. Everyone looked at him strangely. They knew that he was more than a normal man. They knew that he was changed since the Lady of the Land had appeared to him. But not by how much. He was a lòhren now, and he *felt* the land. He sensed the evil in the south as a man sensed a cloud drifting between him and the sun.

At length, he finished speaking. "You should form this kingdom of the five tribes. It is needful. But I will not be king. I am a lòhren, and I have other duties."

At that, they fell silent. Their faces showed they were aghast, but they had no words.

Brand glanced at Taingern and Shorty. They at least did not seem surprised. And strangely, nor did Sighern.

Furthgil found voice for his thoughts. "But lord, everything you have done has … seemed to me to position yourself as king of all the tribes. And we think it a good idea. Will you not reconsider?"

Brand knew he must be decisive here. "I have worked to bring the tribes together. They need a king. But it will not be me. My time in these lands, even the Duthgar, grow short. I am called elsewhere."

Furthgil shook his head sadly. "Then all your labor is in vain. Without you, the tribes will go their separate ways."

"Do you really think so? I don't. The leaders of the five tribes know better than that."

"I fear not," Furthgil replied. "At least, they might know better. But they won't act on that knowledge. Instead, personal ambition will rule. We'll bicker and fight among ourselves to try to take the throne. And when no one can gain acceptance and trust from all the others, we'll go back to chieftainships and tribal lands."

It was Brand's turn to shake his head. "If you cannot rise above that, even seeing the *need* for a king, then you deserve what you get. But there is another choice beside me or bickering among yourselves for ascendancy."

Furthgil accepted the rebuke, for he knew it was true. But still there was a trace of bitterness in his voice when he answered, though Brand thought it stemmed from the truth of his words rather than from anger.

"What other choice can there possibly be?"

"Take for yourself as king one who is not a lord nor even a noble. Choose a man free of ambition. Pick a warrior both wise and courageous. Let him be young, so that he is not steeped in old prejudices, and yet able to learn and appreciate the customs of different tribes. Find someone who will rule all and treat all fairly. Was that not how our ancestors chose their first chieftains?"

Furthgil stroked his beard as though deep in thought, but Brand guessed his mind had already grasped the obvious.

"Who would you propose for such a thing?"

Brand pointed at Sighern. "There is the man I described. Has he not fought for all of us? Has he not shown wit and courage? Does he not still stand before you, even now, carrying the banner of the five tribes? And has he not always been proud to do so?"

The suggestion caused a stir. But Brand removed himself from it. He had done what he could, and now the leaders spoke to Sighern, asking him questions and weighing things in their mind. It would do no harm that the lad had saved Furthgil's life. Furthgil was the most powerful lord left alive among the five tribes. If he accepted Sighern as king, it would sway all the others greatly.

Brand left them to it. His part was done. He had returned to the Duthgar and achieved what he had wanted, but events had grown and shifted.

The Duthgar was not what it was. *He* was not who he had once been. The past was a dream that could be relived

188

only in the mind, and the future was what called him now. It would be bright and new. But also dangerous.

Shorty and Taingern had followed him. They knew better than all others what he had done, and how he felt.

"Where to now?" Shorty asked. "Back to Cardoroth? Elsewhere?"

Brand did not answer immediately. But both his friends saw his gaze turn northward.

Epilogue

Brand did not return to the Duthgar. He wintered in Callenor lands, occupying a hunter's cabin high in a range of forested hills. But he was not alone.

Taingern and Shorty had cabins nearby, though they spent most of their time in his before a hot fire in the hearth during the day or close to the red coals late into the evening.

Sighern had been declared king, and the Banner of Five Tribes went with him wherever he traveled. He had his own bannerman now to carry it. Also, he now wore the Helm of the Duthenor that Brand had given him as well as carrying the Raven Axe of the Callenor.

Even the Waelenor and Druimenor chieftains had acknowledged him as king.

Brand was pleased. And though he enjoyed the solitude of the forested hills, he was not idle. He sent out word for what he intended in spring, and word came back from those who would join him.

The deeps of winter came. And they passed. Snow bound the roads, but still word went to and fro over the lands of the five tribes.

Spring approached, and men gathered. Hardy men and true. Warriors all, fierce and proud. And it mattered not to Brand from which tribe they came, and it mattered not to them.

They were one band now. A thousand strong. Well-armed, provisioned and thirsting for adventure.

Adventure they would have. Upon a spring morning, fine and sunny yet where it had rained during the night, they gathered to leave.

Brand, Taingern and Shorty led them, and they headed northward, leaving their homeland behind. The mountains of the north had always called to Brand, and he never knew why. But he had learned.

Auren Dennath the Halathrin called the mountains. Creatures of evil lurked in the valleys and stalked the high places. But Brand would forge it into a fair kingdom. Or die.

The High Lady had said that he would be a king, and sire kings, and that from his line would spring the hope of the north.

But Brand did not believe in destiny. Nor did the men who went with him. They trusted instead to the courage of their hearts and the true blades they bore.

They would need both.

Thus ends *The Dark God*. It brings the Dark God Rises trilogy to a conclusion. Yet elsewhere in Alithoras ancient evil stirs, and a hero rises to contend with it. Destiny touches him. Prophecy foretold him. But sorcerous forces seek his death.

More will be told in *The Seventh Knight*.

Meanwhile, learn some of Brand's history in *Fate of Kings,* the complete Son of Sorcery trilogy.

FATE OF KINGS

THE COMPLETE SON OF SORCERY TRILOGY

Amazon lists millions of titles, and I'm glad you discovered this one. But if you'd like to know when I release a new book, instead of leaving it to chance, sign up for my newsletter. I'll send you an email on publication.

Yes please! – Go to www.homeofhighfantasy.com and sign up.

No thanks – I'll take my chances.

Dedication

There's a growing movement in fantasy literature. Its name is noblebright, and it's the opposite of grimdark.

Noblebright celebrates the virtues of heroism. It's an old-fashioned thing, as old as the first story ever told around a smoky campfire beneath ancient stars. It's storytelling that highlights courage and loyalty and hope for the spirit of humanity. It recognizes the dark – the dark in us all, and the dark in the villains of its stories. It recognizes death, and treachery and betrayal. But it dwells on none of these things.

I dedicate this book, such as it is, to that which is noblebright. And I thank the authors before me who held the torch high so that I could see the path: J.R.R. Tolkien, C.S. Lewis, Terry Brooks, David Eddings, Susan Cooper, Roger Taylor and many others. I salute you.

And, for a time, I too will hold the torch as high as I can.

Appendix: Encyclopedic Glossary

Note: the glossary of each book in this series is individualized for that book alone. Additionally, there is often historical material provided in its entries for people, artifacts and events that are not included in the main text.

Many races dwell in Alithoras. All have their own language, and though sometimes related to one another the changes sparked by migration, isolation and various influences often render these tongues unintelligible to each other.

The ascendancy of Halathrin culture, combined with their widespread efforts to secure and maintain allies against elug incursions, has made their language the primary means of communication between diverse peoples.

For instance, a merchant of Cardoroth addressing a Duthenor warrior would speak Halathrin, or a simplified version of it, even though their native speeches stem from the same ancestral language.

This glossary contains a range of names and terms. Many are of Halathrin origin, and their meaning is provided. The remainder derive from native tongues and are obscure, so meanings are only given intermittently.

Often, Duthenor names and Halathrin elements are combined. This is especially so for the aristocracy. Few other tribes of men had such long-term friendship with the immortal Halathrin as the Duthenor, and though in this relationship they lost some of their natural culture, they gained nobility and knowledge in return.

List of abbreviations:

Cam. Camar

Comb. Combined

Cor. Corrupted form

Duth. Duthenor

Hal. Halathrin

Kir. Kirsch

Prn. Pronounced

Alithoras: *Hal.* "Silver land." The Halathrin name for the continent they settled after leaving their own homeland. Refers to the extensive river and lake systems they found and their wonder at the beauty of the land.

Anast Dennath: *Hal.* "Stone mountains." Mountain range in northern Alithoras. Source of the river known as the Careth Nien that forms a natural barrier between the lands of the Camar people and the Duthenor and related tribes. Also the location of the Dweorhrealm, the underground stronghold of the dwarven nation.

Aranloth: *Hal.* "Noble might." A lòhren of ancient heritage and friend to Brand.

Arlnoth: *Duth.* "White bear." Chieftain of the Norvinor tribe. Cousin to Furthgil. Intermarriage between the five tribes is common among the nobility. However, the chieftains of the Duthenor avoided it.

Arnhaten: *Kir.* "Disciples." Servants of a magician. One magician usually has many disciples, but only some of these are referred to as "inner door." Inner door disciples receive a full transmission of the master's knowledge. The remainder do not, but they continue to strive to earn the favor of their master. Until they do, they are dispensable.

Attar: *Duth.* "Long-horned ram." A Callenor lord. Related, distantly, to both Arlnoth and Furthgil.

Black Talon: The sign of Unferth's house. Appears on his banner and is his personal emblem. Legend claims the founder of the house in ancient days had the power to transform into a raven. Disguised in this form, and trusted as a magical being, he gave misinformation and ill-advice to the enemies of his people.

Brand: *Duth.* "Torch." An exiled Duthenor tribesman and adventurer. Appointed by the former king of Cardoroth to serve as regent for Prince Gilcarist. By birth, he is the rightful chieftain of the Duthenor people. However, Unferth the Usurper overthrew his father, killing both him and his wife. Brand, only a youth at the time, swore an oath of vengeance.

Breath of the dragon: An ancient saying of Letharn origin. They believed the magic of dragons was the preeminent magic in the world because dragons were creatures able to travel through time. Dragon's breath is known to mean fire, the destructive face of their nature. But the Letharn also believed dragons could breathe mist. This was the healing face of their nature. And the mist-breath of a dragon was held to be able to change destinies and bring good luck. To "ride the dragon's breath" meant that for a period a person was a focal point of time and destiny. The Kar-ahn-hetep peoples hold similar beliefs.

Brodruin: *Duth.* "Dark river." A lord of the Duthgar.

Bruidiger: *Duth.* "Blessed blade." A Norvinor warrior. Brand's father once saved his father's life during a hunting expedition.

Brunhal: *Duth.* "Hallowed woman." Former chieftainess of the Duthenor. Wife to Drunn V, former chieftain of the Duthenor. Mother to Brand. According to Duthenor custom, a chieftain and chieftainess co-ruled.

Callenor: *Duth.* One of several tribes closely related to the Duthenor. This one inhabits lands immediately west of the Duthgar.

Camar: *Cam. Prn.* Kay-mar. A race of interrelated tribes that migrated in two main stages. The first brought them to the vicinity of Halathar, homeland of the immortal Halathrin; in the second, they separated and established cities along a broad stretch of eastern Alithoras. Related to the Duthenor, though far more distantly than the Callenor.

Cardoroth: *Cor. Hal. Comb. Cam.* A Camar city, often called Red Cardoroth. Some say this alludes to the red granite commonly used in the construction of its buildings, others that it refers to a prophecy of destruction.

Careth Nien: *Hal. Prn.* Kareth ny-en. "Great river." Largest river in Alithoras. Has its source in the mountains of Anast Dennath and runs southeast across the land before emptying into the sea. It was over this river (which sometimes freezes along its northern stretches) that the Camar and other tribes migrated into the eastern lands. Much later, Brand came to the city of Cardoroth by one of these ancient migratory routes.

Cartouche: A rectangle, inscribed or engraved, around a royal name. Often referred to by the Kar-ahn-hetep as a Shenna.

Char-harash: *Kir.* "He who destroys by flame." Most exalted of the emperors of the Kirsch, and a magician of great power.

Dragon of the Duthgar: The banner of the chieftains of the Duthenor. Legend holds that an ancient forefather of the line slew a dragon and ate its heart. Dragons are seen by the Duthenor as creatures of ultimate evil, but the consuming of their heart is reputed to pass on wisdom and magic.

Druimenor: One of several tribes closely related to the Duthenor. Named after their first chieftain, Druim. Legend holds he was a brother of Drunn I, first chieftain of the Duthenor.

Drunn: *Duth.* "Man of secrets." Former chieftain of the Duthenor. Husband to Brunhal and father to Brand. Officially known as Drunn V.

Durnheld: *Duth.* "Earth defender – someone who commands a hillfort." A hunter of the Duthgar.

Duthenor: *Duth. Prn.* Dooth-en-or. "The people." A single tribe (or less commonly a group of closely related tribes melded into a larger people at times of war or disaster) who generally live a rustic and peaceful lifestyle. They are breeders of cattle and herders of sheep. However, when need demands they are bold warriors – men and women alike. Until recently, ruled by a usurper who murdered Brand's parents. Brand swore an oath to overthrow the tyrant and avenge his parents. This he has now achieved.

Duthgar: *Duth.* "People spear." The name is taken to mean "the land of the warriors who wield spears."

Elù-haraken: *Hal.* "The shadowed wars." Long ago battles in a time that is become myth to the Duthenor and Camar tribes. A great evil was defeated, though prophecy foretold it would return.

Elùgai: *Hal. Prn.* Eloo-guy. "Shadowed force." The sorcery of an elùgroth.

Erhanu: *Kir.* "The green wanderer." A star. According to ancient stories of the Kar-ahn-hetep, this star was once a god. Other stories, even older, speak of it as the original home of the gods.

Esgallien: *Hal.* "Es – rushing water, gal(en) – green, lien – to cross: place of the crossing onto the green plains." A city established in the south of Alithoras. Named after the nearby ford.

Ferstellenpund: *Duth.* "Fer – to bring, stellen – peace, pund – sacred enclosure." A sacred tarn within the Duthgar and revered by the Duthenor. Each of the five tribes conducts rituals at such a place within their lands.

Furthgil: *Duth.* "Head warrior – a commander of an armed troop." The preeminent surviving lord of the Callenor tribe. Related to some houses of Duthenor nobility, though not to Brand.

Garvengil: *Duth.* "Warrior of the woods." A lord of the Duthgar.

God-king: See Char-harash.

Gormengil: *Duth.* "Warrior of the storm." Nephew of Unferth. Rightful heir to the Callenor chieftainship, until Brand defeated him in single combat.

Halathrin: *Hal.* "People of Halath." A race named after an honored lord who led an exodus of his people to the land of Alithoras in pursuit of justice, having sworn to defeat a great evil. They are human, though of fairer form, greater skill and higher culture than ordinary men. They possess a unity of body, mind and spirit that enables insight and endurance beyond the native races of Alithoras. Said to be immortal, but killed in great numbers during their conflicts in ancient times with the evil they sought to destroy. Those conflicts are collectively known as the Shadowed Wars.

Haldring: *Duth.* "White blade – a sword that flashes in the sun." A shield-maiden. Killed in the first great battle between the forces of Brand and the usurper.

Hathulf: *Duth.* "Honey hunter – generally interpreted to mean a bear, but can also refer to a brave warrior." A lord of the Callenor.

High Way: An ancient road longer than the Duthgar, but well preserved in that land. Probably of Letharn origin and used to speed troops to battle.

Horta: *Kir.* "Speech of the acacia tree." It is believed among the Kar-ahn-hetep that the acacia tree possesses magical properties that aid discourse between the realms of men and gods. Horta is a name that recurs among families noted for producing elite magicians.

Hralfling: *Duth.* "The shower of sparks off two sword blades striking." An elderly lord of the Callenor.

Hruidgar: *Duth.* "Ashwood spear." A Duthenor hunter.

Jarch-elrah: *Kir.* "The hunter that laughs as it kills." A god of the Kar-ahn-hetep. The form he chooses is human, but jackal headed. Reputed to be mad, but the minds and intentions of gods are not easily interpreted by humans. Some ancient magicians contend his madness is a ploy to assist him in remaining neutral in the disputes of the gods and enables him to avoid aligning himself with the various factions.

Kar-ahn-hetep: *Kir.* "The children of the thousand stars." A race of people that vied for supremacy in ancient times with the Letharn. Their power was ultimately broken, their empire destroyed. But a residual population survived and defied outright annihilation by their conquerors. They believe their empire will one day rise again to rule the world. The kar-ahn element of their name means the "thousand stars" but also "the lights that never die."

Kar-fallon: *Kir.* "Death city." A great city of the Kar-ahn-hetep that served as their principal religious focus. Their magician-priests conducted the great rites of their nation in its sacred temples.

Kar-karmun: *Kir.* "Death-life – the runes of life and death." A means of divination that distills the wisdom and worldview of the Kar-ahn-hetep civilization.

Kirsch: See Kar-ahn-hetep.

Lady of the Land: The spirit of the land. It is she whom lòhrens serve, though her existence is seldom discussed. It is said she favored Drunn I, and came to him in his greatest hour of need during the elù-haraken, advising him how to defeat his enemies and lead the five tribes to the lands they now inhabit.

Letharn: *Hal.* "Stone raisers. Builders." A race of people that in antiquity conquered most of Alithoras. Now, only faint traces of their civilization endure.

Light of Kar-fallon: See Char-harash.

Lòhren: *Hal. Prn.* Ler-ren. "Knowledge giver – a counselor." Other terms used by various nations include wizard, druid and sage.

Lòhrengai: *Hal. Prn.* Ler-ren-guy. "Lòhren force." Enchantment, spell or use of mystic power. A manipulation and transformation of the natural energy inherent in all things. Each use takes something from the user. Likewise, some part of the transformed energy infuses them. Lòhrens use it sparingly, elùgroths indiscriminately.

Lord of the Ten Armies: See Char-harash.

Magic: Mystic power. See lòhrengai and elùgai.

Murlek: A star revered by the Kar-ahn-hetep. Also the sign of their healers. A star is engraved upon their doors and on their medical instruments.

Norhanu: *Kir.* "Serrated blade." A psychoactive herb.

Norvinor: *Duth.* One of several tribes closely related to the Duthenor. This one inhabits lands west of the Callenor.

Ossar the Great: Sometimes called a star, but in reality a planet. Said to be a dead god. On occasion, claimed to be the deceased father of all the gods. At least, the more ancient stories invoke this status for him.

Pennling Palace: A fortress in the Duthgar. Named after an ancient hero of the Duthenor. In truth, constructed by the Letharn and said to be haunted by the spirits of the dead. At certain nights, especially midwinter and midsummer, legend claims the spirits are visible manning the walls and fighting a great battle.

Pennling Path: Etymology obscure. Pennling was an ancient hero of the Duthenor. Some say he built the road in the Duthgar known as the High Way. This is not true, but one legend holds that he traveled all its length in one night on a milk-white steed to confront an attacking army by himself. It is said that his ghost may yet be seen racing along the road on his steed when the full moon hangs above the Duthgar.

Raithlin: *Hal.* "Range and report people." A scouting and saboteur organization. They derive from ancient contact with the Halathrin.

Rite of Resurrection: The highest magic of the magicians of the Kar-ahn-hetep. According to legend, said only to have been successfully performed once. This was during the great wars against the Letharn empire.

Ruler of the Thousand Stars: See Char-harash.

Runes of Life and Death: See Kar-karmun.

Shadowed wars: See Elù-haraken.

Shemfal: *Kir.* "Cool shadows gliding over the hot waste – dusk." One of the greater gods of the Kar-ahn-hetep. Often depicted as a mighty man, bat winged and bat headed. Ruler of the underworld. Given a wound in battle with other gods that does not heal and causes him to limp.

Shenti: A type of kilt worn by the Kar-ahn-hetep.

Shorty: A former Durlindrath (chief bodyguard of the king of Cardoroth). Friend to Brand. His proper name is Lornach.

Sighern: *Duth.* "Battle leader." A youth of the Duthgar.

Su-sarat: *Kir.* "The serpent that lures." One of the greater gods of the Kar-ahn-hetep. Her totem is the desert puff adder that lures prey by flicking either its tongue or tail. Called also the Trickster. It was she who gave the god Shemfal his limp.

Tanata: *Kir.* "Stalker of the desert at night." A disciple of Horta.

Taingern: *Cam.* "Still sea," or "calm waters." A former Durlindrath (chief bodyguard of the king of Cardoroth). Friend to Brand.

Thurlnoth: *Duth.* "Charging bear." A lord of the Norvinor. Son of Arlnoth.

Tinwellen: *Cam.* "Sun of the earth – gold." Daughter of a prosperous merchant of Cardoroth.

Unferth: *Duth.* "Hiss of arrows." The name is sometimes interpreted to mean "whispered counsels that lead to war." Usurper of the chieftainship of the Duthenor. Rightful chieftain of the Callenor. Slain by Gormengil in single combat.

Ùhrengai: *Hal. Prn.* Er-ren-guy. "Original force." The primordial force that existed before substance or time.

Uzlakah: A tree of the southern deserts of Alithoras. Valued not just for its shade, but also the long and nutritious pods it provides.

Waelenor: One of several tribes closely related to the Duthenor. Founded by their original chieftain, Wael, brother of Drunn I.

Wena: *Kir.* "The kestrel that hovers." Leader of a Kar-ahn-hetep army.

Wizard: See lòhren.

Wizard-priest: The priests of the Letharn. Possessors of mighty powers of magic. Forerunners to the order of lòhrens.

About the author

I'm a man born in the wrong era. My heart yearns for faraway places and even further afield times. Tolkien had me at the beginning of *The Hobbit* when he said, ". . . one morning long ago in the quiet of the world . . ."

Sometimes I imagine myself in a Viking mead-hall. The long winter night presses in, but the shimmering embers of a log in the hearth hold back both cold and dark. The chieftain calls for a story, and I take a sip from my drinking horn and stand up . . .

Or maybe the desert stars shine bright and clear, obscured occasionally by wisps of smoke from burning camel dung. A dry gust of wind marches sand grains across our lonely campsite, and the wayfarers about me stir restlessly. I sip cool water and begin to speak.

I'm a storyteller. A man to paint a picture by the slow music of words. I like to bring faraway places and times to life, to make hearts yearn for something they can never have, unless for a passing moment.